THE CASE OF THE KEY LIME CRIMES

A Gossip Cozy Mystery Book 2

ROSIE A. POINT

 Created with Vellum

YOU'RE INVITED!

Hi there, reader!

I'd like to formally invite you to join my awesome community of readers. We love to chat about cozy mysteries, cooking, and pets.

It's super fun because I get to share chapters from yet-to-be-released books, fun recipes, pictures, and do giveaways with the people who enjoy my stories the most.

So whether you're a new reader or you've been

enjoying my stories for a while, you can catch up with other like-minded readers, and get lots of cool content by visiting my website at *www.rosiepointbooks.com* and signing up for my mailing list.

Or simply search for me on *www.bookbub.com* and follow me there.

I look forward to getting to know you better.

Let's get into the story!

Yours,
Rosie

MEET THE CHARACTERS

Charlie Smith (Mission)—An ex-spy, Charlie's lives and works in her grandmother's inn in Gossip, Texas, as a server, maid, and assistant. With her particular set of skills and spunky attitude, she's become Gossip's "fixer" thanks to her previous involvement in solving murder mysteries.

Georgina Franklin (Mission)—Charlie's super-spy grandmother who raised her. Georgina (or Gamma, as Charlie calls her) is the most decorated spy in the history of the

NSIB. She's retired, but still as smart and spry as ever.

Lauren Harris—The happy-go-lucky chef at the Gossip Inn. A master baker, she's always got delicious cupcakes prepared for the inn's lunches and dinners. She's jolly, with bright red hair she wears in pigtails.

Cocoa Puff—Georgina's chocolate brown cat. He's friendly as can be with people he trusts. Often sleeps on Charlie's bed and accompanies her around the inn, helping her dust the various trinkets and tables.

Sunlight—Charlie's newly adopted cat and co-sleuth. A ginger kitty with an adventurous spirit. He loves to get up to mischief in the inn and always has Charlie's back.

Jessie Belle-Blue—Jessie is Georgina's worst nightmare. As the owner of the local cattery and now, a guesthouse, she hates the fact that Georgina has opened a kitten foster center in direct competition. Will do whatever it takes to come out on top.

Detective Aaron Goode—The new tough detective in town. He's handsome, with dark hair, a strong jawline, and unflinching determination to get to the bottom of things. He doesn't appreciate interference.

Glendaree Bijon—The winner of last year's Tri-State Baking Competition. She's ostentatious and believes that she's the rightful winner of this year's competition before it has even taken place. A trying woman to talk to. Loves wearing kaftans and heavy makeup.

Brenda Tippett—A local librarian, Brenda makes friends easily and adores reading books. She was runner-up in last year's Tri-State Baking Competition and believes that this is her year! She's a passionate baker.

Marie Tippett—Brenda's sister from the big city. She doesn't like having to handle her little sister's business and thinks she's far too important to be wasting time in a small town like Gossip.

Colton Harrison—A local baker who works hard to ensure he's always at top of his game. Determined to win the prize at the baking competition this year, he's been working several jobs so that he has money for ingredients.

Kayla Wren—A baker with a shady past. She's incredibly shy and doesn't want anyone to go poking their noses in her business. Especially since she's got so much to hide. Pretty but mousy and young.

Norman Sweet—Brenda's boyfriend. He works at the library, or so he says, and leaves the house early every morning. Has a tendency to do his gardening barefoot and likes to wear tank tops.

Misty Primrose—Brenda's neighbor. She's a freelance graphic designer who spends a lot of time indoors and working from home. Potentially deficient in Vitamin D.

Deirdre Hardecki—A local gossip and entrant in the baking contest. She makes it her business to know everyone's business, whether they like it or not. She's got a serious case of motor mouth.

1

"She crept up the stairs, her heart pounding against the inside of her throat, and inched toward the door." I pressed my fingers against the bottom of my paperback, pinning it open while I read to Sunlight and Cocoa Puff. "It was ajar, and a sickly sweetness drifted out toward her. A smell she recognized. One she had hoped she would never encounter again." I paused for effect.

The inn's two resident cats, Cocoa Puff, the veteran, chocolate in color and as adorable as the day I'd met him, and Sunlight, my new boisterous kitty cat, studied me with bright yellow eyes, seated beside each other at the foot of my bed.

"The odor was so foul she pressed a hand to her mouth, willing her nausea away, yet she was drawn onward. Her shoes scuffed on the creaking floorboards."

Cocoa yawned and proceeded to lick the front of his chest, pulling faces only a cat could while doing so. Sunlight let out the tiniest of meows then curled up into a ball, purring softly.

"Oh, come on." I flapped a hand in their direction. "We're reaching the climax. She's about to find out who's been murdering the townsfolk! You know, you two need a literary education. It's nearly Halloween." That wasn't technically true. Halloween was two months away, but as one of my favorite holidays, I was ready to start the celebrations early.

Anything to spice things up a bit at the inn.

It had been surprisingly boring here of

late. Apart from the usual cat and guest herding, the chef's mood swings as her due date approached, and the upcoming opening of the ghost tours at the Gossip Inn, there had been nothing to write home about.

Then again, Gossip was my home and the only person I'd write to was my grandmother who owned the inn.

Sunlight gave another purring meow. Cocoa Puff laid down, lifted a leg and set to work cleaning his private area.

"You two are hopeless," I sighed. "It's past time we get in a spooky mood around here. I'm going to talk to Georgina about putting up the Halloween decorations early."

Something had to give. As an ex-spy, I couldn't stand the quiet for much longer.

I continued reading. "Rumelda pressed a hand to the door and immediately withdrew it. The wood was ice cold. Her breath misted in front of her face, and, not for the first time, she considered turning back. But the mystery had dug its bloodied claws into her flesh." I shook my head at the cats. "Come on. This is good stuff. I can't believe you're not as spooked out as I am."

A couple of years ago, the prospect of talking to cats and expecting them to understand me would've made me spit out my protein bar. Now, I could barely get through the day without a cupcake and a chat with Cocoa and Sunlight.

I wasn't even mad about it.

"Rumelda took a breath, pushed the door open. The room was dark, but not dark enough to hide the horror within. A scream tore from her throat and—"

A high-pitched shriek broke the silence in the inn.

I stiffened.

Wait a second. Was that my imagination or—?

But no. Both Cocoa and Sunlight were up. Sunlight stared at the bedroom door, and Cocoa jumped off the bed and darted underneath it.

A second scream, shrill and terrified, rose

from below. I glanced at the alarm clock on my bedside table—03:00 a.m..

I jumped out of bed, opened my bedside table drawer, lifted the false bottom, and extracted my Sig Sauer from within. I strapped it to my side, slipped on my white, cotton robe, and exited my bedroom.

Though I'd be the first to admit that I hadn't been a particularly good spy, my training had kicked in. The slightest movement drew my attention, and my breathing was calm, my gaze focused. I left one hand on my weapon, ready to draw it at a moment's notice.

A figure glided down the hall toward me in white striped PJs. My grandmother carried her shotgun out in the open. "Awake so late, Charlotte?" Her prim British accent was pronounced.

I didn't bother asking Gamma why she was up at this hour. She barely slept, possibly because she'd seen too much as one of the NSIB's most decorated spies.

"I was reading. You heard the screams too?"

"I believe everyone heard the screams." Indeed, a rumbling of chatter came from the floor below us.

We made our way down the stairs together. I tied my robe closed, letting Gamma walk with her shotgun out. It was expected of Georgina Franklin to wield a shotgun at odd hours of the day and night—she'd acquired somewhat of a reputation—but I was the "meek maid" at the inn.

"Who screamed?" A man's voice from the first floor landing. "What's going on?"

"I heard it too." A woman.

"This is ridiculous. Some of us need our beauty sleep."

"Mommy, I'm scared."

"It's OK, Charity, darling. Everything will be just fine. It's probably something to do with the ghost tours, you know. It's almost Halloween."

"But in the middle of the night? This isn't what I'm paying for."

Gamma reached the first floor landing ahead of me and stopped abruptly. "Attention," she said, raising her voice. "All guests are required to meet in the dining room, tout suite."

The guests from the first floor stared at her in varying states of shock and horror. "But what is it?" A man asked. "What's going on?"

"We're not sure as yet," Gamma replied. "Rest assured, your questions will be answered in due course." She ignored the grumbling from the guests and turned to me. "Charlotte, proceed up to the other floors and execute Contingency Plan 4."

"Copy," I murmured.

After the last "mystery" at the Gossip Inn —of which there had been many—Gamma and I had come up with several emergency plans to keep the guests protected and danger at a minimum.

You'd think that living in a small town in Texas wouldn't provide too much danger, but with our collective histories... well, it looked like I was about to get that excitement I'd been after.

I hurried up the stairs and did as Gamma had instructed, collecting the guests from the second and third floors, ushering them downstairs and into the dining room. Apart from the plans we'd put in place, Gamma had also installed a new security system. Cameras watched the exterior of the inn but not the halls to protect the guests' privacy.

"This is everyone, I think," I said, entering the dining room.

The lights were on and bleary-eyed guests conversed or glared around at the room and each other. Most of the anger was directed at Gamma.

"What's going on?" a man yelled, over the noise. "We deserve answers. Who was scream-ing? What is—?"

Gamma lifted her pump shotgun and cocked it in one hand. She was in her late sixties, but she was hard as nails, strong as steel. "Quiet," she said, calmly. "Your questions will be answered soon."

"Do *not* tell him to be quiet." A woman rose from a table near the dining room windows, and I groaned inwardly.

Not her again.

Glendaree Bijon.

She had been giving us trouble ever since she'd arrived last week, and she stood with her fists on her hips, staring us down. Glendaree wore a silken robe over an equally silky nightgown, both gold in color. She had pinned up her gray hair in a fountain of curls, and she wore severe eye makeup.

Had she splashed it on before coming down for the emergency meeting? Or did she wear eyeshadow to bed? Both options disturbed me equally.

"Miss Bijon, please, take a seat," Gamma said, calmly. "We're going to get to the bottom of what's going on, shortly."

"It's Mrs. Bijon to you," she snapped. "Just

because my husband is gone doesn't mean you can call me whatever you like. I should report you for—"

A howl rose outside and most of the guests gasped.

It had sounded like a dog or a—

"Werewolf!" The scream came from behind us.

Lauren, the usually cheerful chef, stood beneath the dining room's archway, one hand on her pregnant stomach, the other on her head. She was pale, sweat shimmering on her upper lip.

"Lauren!" I rushed to her side, taking hold of the underside of her arm. "Are you OK? What happened?"

Gamma joined us as chaos erupted in the dining room. "Was that you screaming earlier?"

Lauren nodded. "I think I'm going to faint."

Carefully, Gamma and I escorted the chef, her usually vibrant red hair hanging limp against her cheeks, into the inn's kitchen. We seated her at the table and I made quick work of getting her a tall glass of water and one of her delicious cupcakes.

Lauren ate the sugary treat greedily and color returned to her cheeks. She sipped the water. "I'm s-sorry," she said. "I hope I didn't scare you."

"What happened, Lauren?" Gamma stroked her back, standing behind the chef's chair.

"It was the craziest thing. I—"

"What is the meaning of this madness?" Glendaree Bijon had followed us back to the kitchen. She pointed a bejewelled finger—seriously, bejeweled at this time of night—at Lauren. "I demand compensation for the disturbance of my beauty sleep. You will eject this cretin from the inn at once."

I rounded on her, but Gamma shot me a look. "Mrs. Bijon," she said, "there appears to have been a serious emergency with one of our staff members. We apologize for any inconvenience caused. Charlotte will escort you and the other guests back to your rooms." Gamma had assessed the situation and determined there wasn't an imminent threat.

"Right this way, Mrs. Bijon," I said, doing as my grandmother had instructed.

Glendaree drew herself up straight, clutching the sides of her golden robe. "I expect compensation," she growled. "The Tri-State Baking Competition is at the end of the week, and I need my beauty sleep if I'm going to win again."

"Of course," I replied. "My sincerest apologies, Mrs. Bijon." Words had never tasted as bitter. Charlotte Mission, the spy, wanted to pull that golden robe over Glendaree's head and run her into a wall. Charlotte Smith, the maid, wouldn't so much as hiss at a mouse.

I spent the next thirty minutes apologizing to guests, escorting them back to their rooms, checking all the exits were locked, and checking on the kittens and assistant in the kitten foster center attached to the inn.

Finally, I joined Gamma and Lauren in the kitchen.

The chef talked animatedly. "—didn't mean to disturb anyone."

"All right," I said, plopping into a chair beside her and grabbing a cupcake from the center plate on the table. "Would someone like to fill me in on what that was about? Because it took all my energy not to stuff Mrs. Bijon into a closet on the way up the stairs."

"I'm so sorry, Charlotte," Lauren said. "I didn't mean to disturb anyone."

"So, what happened?" I asked.

"It's quite the tale," Gamma said, from where she stood, preparing a pot of coffee. Apparently, we'd decided we weren't going back to bed. Then again, it was past 04:00 a.m., so what was the point? We'd have to wake up soon to start the morning prep for breakfast.

Lauren stroked her belly. "I wanted to

come out to the inn early today, you see, because I couldn't sleep, and I'm kind of nervous for the baking competition. I thought I'd get a headstart on the preparations this morning. Maybe trial a new version of the key lime pie I want to make for the main event."

"OK? And the screaming?"

"Right. So, this is where it gets strange," Lauren said. "I arrived at the inn like normal, and I was just going to open the side door of the kitchen, there." She pointed to the back door. "When I heard... this... oh my, it was horrible." Her southern accent grew particularly strong.

"What was it?"

"I heard this shuffling in the darkness behind me. I turned around, thinking maybe it was the new gardener or just a guest or a small critter or something, and that was when I saw it."

"Saw what?"

"The werewolf."

I frowned, glancing up at my grandmother.

She shrugged.

Lauren was heavily into superstitions. She believed in ghosts and the paranormal, and now, werewolves. I didn't buy it. Call me a skeptic, but there was usually a good explanation for things that went bump in the night.

In my world, those bumps were often made by men with guns. Or women with guns. Evil didn't have a gender.

"A werewolf," I repeated, drily.

"Well, yeah! I know a wolf when I see one. This one was huge, and grey, and it looked at me with this evil gleam in its eyes, and that was when I screamed. I couldn't get the door open, so I screamed again. I eventually got inside, and then I... well, I sat down at the table, and I fell asleep."

"You fell asleep?" My eyebrows lifted. "After that?"

"I was exhausted," Lauren said. "I think it was all the shock and fear and stuff. I just fell asleep. And then I woke up and I heard the noise from the dining room and it came rushing back and I just had to tell someone and—"

"It's OK." I patted Lauren on the shoulder. Was it normal for pregnant women to have hallucinations when they were close to their due date?

Or she saw a big dog in the inn's back yard.

"Don't bother with any of this today, Lauren." Gamma set down a cup of hot chocolate in front of the chef. "You should focus on your practice for the Tri-State Baking Competition this week."

"You're right," Lauren said. "I need to bring my A-game. That Glendaree Bijon won't go down without a fight."

Their conversation wandered to baking, and I tuned most of it out. A part of me wanted to go out there and see if I could find evidence of this "werewolf", but we had prep to get to.

Still, I couldn't help glancing at the back door. It had been a while since there'd been a good mystery to solve.

2

Later that morning...

"I need to sit down for a minute," Lauren said, grasping the back of a kitchen chair. "Could you watch the bacon for me, Charlie?"

"Sure thing." I took my place in front of the stovetop and did exactly what she'd asked of me. I watched the bacon. I didn't touch it or even breathe too heavily near the pan. As experience had shown, whenever I did anything that wasn't under Lauren's direction, the breakfast, lunch or dinner would flop.

And it wasn't like I'd been trying to sabotage anything either. It just... happened. Cooking wasn't my forte. But I had a certain je nais se quois when it came to dusting.

The bacon sizzled in the pan, releasing its delicious salty flavor. It was nearly time to serve the guests, most of whom had arrived grumpy after the night's interruption. Lauren was in good spirits, however, and that was all that mattered to me.

"All right," the chef said, pushing up from her chair. "Let's finish this breakfast."

"Are you feeling OK? Remember, Georgina said you shouldn't strain yourself." I referred to my grandmother as Georgina in front of Lauren, even though she was the only person in Gossip who knew the truth about our familial relationship.

"I'm fine." Lauren flapped her hands then picked up her spatula and started flipping the bacon slices in the pan. "Y'all have got to stop worrying about me so much."

"Forgive me, Laur, but you did see a werewolf this morning." I tacked a silent "allegedly" at the end of that sentence.

"I know, but as long as we keep the doors locked today we'll be fine," she said, not hearing the sarcasm in my tone or choosing to ignore it. "Besides, werewolves only come out at night under a full moon. There's only a couple of days before the new moon anyway. And there's plenty of silverware in the kitchen too."

"Silverware?"

"To ward off the werewolf. Aw, come on, Charlie, surely you know that werewolves can't stand silver?"

"Right. Sure. Good thing we're stocked up on garlic for the cannelloni too."

"That's for vampires," Lauren said, waving her spatula at me. "Really, Charlie, I know you're, uh, experienced when it comes to looking after yourself, but you've got to pay attention to details like that. Imagine. Thrusting a clove of garlic at a werewolf..." She tittered as if it was the funniest thing she'd ever heard.

"Yeah. Crazy." I didn't mind Lauren's eccentricities. She was a lovely person and a good friend. Besides, I was pretty sure the crazy fog would lift after she had her second child.

Lauren was huge in that bountiful, "my ribs hurt, get this thing out of me" way, and due any day.

"Just take it easy." I pressed the point. "We don't want you doing anything that could harm—"

My grandmother entered the kitchen, slapping a rolled up copy of *The Gossip Rag*, our least favorite local newspaper, against her palm. "She's done it again."

"What, Jacinta?" The editor of the magazine had a penchant for picking on The Gossip Inn and my grandmother.

"No, the other one."

"Belle-Blue?" I asked.

Gamma hissed at the mention of her arch enemy's last name. "Precisely," she said, once she'd regained control. "Just look at this. Can you believe it?" She slapped the newspaper down on the kitchen table.

Lauren and I walked over to check it out.

Meet the judges of the Tri-State Baking Competition! Including one of Gossip's finest!

"Gossip's finest?" I raised an eyebrow.

"Do *not* get me started," Gamma replied, though, technically she'd started moments ago. "That idiot Belle-Blue is going to be judging the competition. Why in the world would they want her to judge a baking competition? The woman couldn't bake a trifle!"

"Do you bake trifles?" I wrinkled my nose.

"No. That's the point," Gamma said.

"Oh no." Lauren lifted the paper, her eyes darting back and forth as she read the article. "It says she was chosen out of a host of nominees to be a local judge. They're saying she's known for being the owner of a successful inn."

Gamma's complexion went from its usual porcelain to boiled beetroot. "Successful?"

"Well, shoot, if they were looking for a successful business owner, they should've just come to you, Georgina," Lauren said.

That, of course, didn't help my grand-mother's demeanor. "I'm sorry," I said. "This is not ideal."

"Not ideal! It's a mockery, is what it is. Why on earth would they choose that troglodyte to judge the competition? It doesn't make any sense."

"Maybe she paid her way in," I replied. "You never know."

"No. That pashmina-wearing fool doesn't have enough money for that. Unless..."

"Unless?"

"Her husband," Gamma sighed. "Belle-Blue's new husband has money. You might be right, Charlotte. But that doesn't make me feel any better. This will only go to her head.

And she'll use every bit of attention she gets to discredit me."

Lauren chewed on her bottom lip. "I hope this doesn't mean what I think it does." Tears welled in her eyes—her emotions were hormonally heightened. "She's going to judge my entry harshly. She'll make it so the other judges give me low scores and then I'll be out. Oh, I just knew something like this would happen. I knew it."

"I'll strangle her," Gamma growled.

"Now, now, everyone relax," I said.

It wasn't like my grandmother to get this angry, but Belle-Blue had a gift for getting under her skin.

"Don't give Belle-Blue room in your head." I put my arm around Lauren's shoulder and gave her a squeeze. "Come on. Let's finish up breakfast."

"Thanks, Charlie, you're too sweet." Lauren wiped her tears with her apron then returned to the stove.

Gamma marched over to the countertop

where warm dishes awaited, and I followed her. I couldn't help wondering how Belle-Blue had done it. Interesting. That brought the count of mysteries for the week up to two.

First, the werewolf, and now—

A yell, throaty and full of rage, sounded from the dining room.

3

"What was that?" Lauren asked, pausing as she dished bacon onto a silver platter.

"I believe that's what they, in the business, call a rage-filled scream," I replied, heading for the swinging kitchen doors with their porthole windows.

"There's been a lot of screaming the past few days. I hope it's not catching," Gamma put in, following me out into the dining area.

As usual, the room was packed with the

Gossip Inn's guests. But unlike usual, a woman stood in the center of the room, her fists on her hips, glaring around as if she was a queen who had been offended by her loyal subjects.

Glendaree Bijon in high dudgeon. Man, I'd had a feeling that this week was about to take a turn for the worse.

"You're lucky I don't report you all to the police," she said, casting her arms wide. Today, she wore a shimmering bronze kaftan, her hair curled tight against her scalp. Bangles clacked up and down her arms and oversized earrings tugged on her earlobes. "If you don't own up to being a witness to this crime, I will ensure that you are prosecuted as an accessory!"

"Mrs. Bijon," Gamma said, and that practiced calm was back in her tone. "You appear to be disturbing my guests. Kindly resume your seat. Breakfast is about to begin."

"How can I possibly eat breakfast when this horror is unfolding before my eyes?" She gave Gamma an imperious stare.

"I assure you, there's nothing to worry about, Mrs. Bijon," Gamma said. "There are no 'werewolves' on the premises and—"

"I'm not talking about werewolves," Glendaree scoffed. "My recipe book was stolen two days ago and no one has done anything about it. I demand justice!" She glanced at me, surreptitiously, likely believing that the look would go unnoticed. But I caught it.

Mrs. Bijon was up to something. *Color me intrigued.*

Gamma had noticed too and pressed two fingers to my elbow, indicating that I should take the lead.

"Your recipe book was stolen?" I asked.

"Yes," Glendaree said, lowering her voice. "As last year's winner of the Tri-State Baking Competition, my competitors will stop at nothing to prevent me from claiming the top spot again this year. That recipe book was my secret weapon. A Bijon family heirloom containing my winning recipe for key lime pie. It's unbearable that it's fallen into the hands of a thief. An enemy. Someone who wants to see me fail."

"I'm sorry about that, Mrs. Bijon. But this is the first we're hearing of it," I said. "Why didn't you tell us that your recipe book was stolen sooner?"

Glendaree's tortured expression shifted to one of shock for a millisecond then back again. *Oh, you're hiding something all right.* "Because I thought the police would be able to handle it, but Detective Goode at the station has proven to be an inept fool. I took my problem to them and he was assigned to my case. He has done *nothing* to find the perpetrator. Can you believe that?"

I shook my head but didn't answer.

Glendaree stared at me, expectantly, but I waited. The longer I remained silent, the higher the pressure weighed on her to fill in the gaps.

"If I don't find that recipe book, I'll just,

well, I don't know what I'll do. I need it to perform in the Tri-State Baking Competition." She withdrew a flowery handkerchief from her kaftan sleeve like a magician. She dabbed underneath either eye.

"I wish we could help you, but—" I started.

"You can!" Glendaree practically yelled it. "I know I'm not a resident of this town, but in the short time I've been here, I've heard a few things."

"Such as?" Gamma asked.

"My friends in town tell me that if I have a problem, then you, young lady, are the woman I should talk to. Is that correct?"

Now, how on earth had she learned that within a span of a week? I was Gossip's "fixer", the person people came to when they needed a problem handled without police involvement. But the folks in town, while they enjoyed gossiping, tended toward keeping that gossip in town circles. They excluded outsiders. And this was Glendaree's first time in town.

Something's fishy about this.

It had been so quiet lately. Any opportunity to annoy Detective Goode was also a plus. The new officer had gotten on my nerves more than once already.

"Sure," I said, at last.

Glendaree clasped her hands together, smushing her moist handkerchief between her palms. "I will pay you for your services, of course. Whichever rate you think is fair. All I care about are results, you know. I want the perpetrator tracked down and brought to justice. And I need my recipe book back desperately. The competition is mere days away. Please, please, you've got to help me, Miss Smith."

No way had Glendaree remembered my name. Every bit of this was suspicious, and I lived for that, if I was honest with myself.

I considered the proposition, aware of my grandmother's presence at my side. She was calm, watching, but I knew her well by now. Gamma would want me to check this out, if only to prove that Glendaree was up to something.

And while I was at it, I could find out how Jessie Belle-Blue had gotten on the judging panel. Between baking and the new ghost tours set to start this week, there wasn't much else to do. Besides, kibble wasn't cheap, and any extra money I brought in would help my grandmother.

"All right," I said, quietly, aware that some of the other guests were watching and desperately trying to overhear the conversation. "I'll take your case. We'll talk about it after breakfast."

"Oh, thank you so much, Miss Smith. Thank you!" She took my hand and clutched it, squeezing it tight. "I just knew you would find it in your heart to help me." She fluttered her long lashes at me before tottering off to the table in front of the dining room windows.

"I assume you're going to find out why she's acting so strangely," Gamma said.

"You can count on that." We headed back to the kitchen to fetch the serving dishes and start the breakfast service. Questions broiled in my mind.

❧ 4 ❧

After breakfast...

"Shouldn't we have this conversation in privacy?" Glendaree asked, patting her gray curls and casting her disparaging gaze at my grandmother.

I'd requested that Gamma sit in on my interview with the new "client" to put more pressure on Glendaree. I had my suspicions about her already, and as a spy, I'd learned to pick up on strange vibes. And on the weird vibe-o-meter, Glendaree was hitting a solid 10.

"We are in privacy." I gestured to the egg-yolk yellow walls in the dining room. The guests had left the gorgeous glossy tables with their crystal vase centerpieces over twenty minutes ago.

"I mean..." Glendaree nodded to my grandmother. "Is this how you usually conduct business?"

I withdrew a pen from my apron along with my mini-notepad and tapped them both on the table. "I'm sorry, Mrs. Bijon, I was under the impression that you needed my help?"

"I do."

"Then surely you trust me to do a good job," I said.

"Yes. Of course. I believe you'll find the maniac who took my beloved recipe book."

That's a strange way to put it. "Then you'll have to trust my processes," I said. "Including involving Mrs. Franklin in this conversation."

"Fine," she said, after a beat. "But you have to admit that it's rather strange."

As strange as wearing a bronze kaftan to breakfast?

Then again, who was I to judge? I was hardly fashion forward. "Now," I said, opening my notepad and uncapping my pen. "Talk to me about what's going on. You said your recipe book was stolen two days ago?"

"Yes." Glendaree allowed herself a final shift of eyes toward my silent grandmother. "Yes, two days ago. From my very room in this very inn."

"And you're staying in the Lavender Room," I said. "Is that correct?"

"Yes. Yes it is."

"When did you first notice that the recipe book was missing?"

Glendaree interlaced her fingers and rested them on top of the table. "It was when I got back from dinner at the Hungry Steer, this horrible little barnyard themed restaurant. I don't recommend going there." She shuddered, delicately. "I returned and my bed-room door was ajar. I didn't think anything of it until I found that my dressing table had been opened and my recipe book was missing. I immediately reported it to the police."

I noted down the information, keeping my private thoughts from the page. She hadn't thought anything of her door being ajar? Suspicious.

"All right," I said. "And what did the police say?"

"That they would get to the bottom of it. But they refused to take fingerprints. They didn't even come to the crime scene, for heaven's sake. I'm starting to think they aren't taking this seriously."

Gossip was a small town. There wasn't much going on apart from the occasional theft, domestic dispute, and petty crime. A guy like Goode, who liked to get involved in everything, would've been here in a heartbeat if it gave him an opportunity to investigate *something*.

And to annoy me. Slow heat crept up my throat. The last time I'd talk to Detective Aaron Goode had been *different* to say the least.

"What's wrong? You've gone red."

"Nothing," I said. "Back to the recipe book. You're saying it was stolen because of the Tri-State Baking Competition, yes?"

"What other reason could there possibly be? I'm the star baker. The woman who won the last competition, and people *know* that I keep my best recipes in that book. They'd do anything to get their hands on it if it meant sabotaging me."

"Right. So it stands to reason that the thief is one of the contest's entrants, correct?"

"That's what I believe."

"Then who do you think might've done this?" I asked.

Glendaree immediately started listing off names. "There's Kaley Wren, Colton Harrison, and my main suspect," she said, "is Brenda Tippett. The runner-up in last year's competition. Mean little witch of a woman who always wears mauve. Mauve!"

"Brenda's a Gossip resident," Gamma said, quietly. "She lives on Brewer Lane."

I noted the names down, drawing a line under each of them, and adding the extra information for Brenda Tippett. "Is there anything else you can tell me about that night? Anything unusual that happened?"

"No," Glendaree said. "That's everything I can think of. Please, you've got to find my recipe book. If someone uses my key lime pie recipe to win, I'll just die!"

A flair for the dramatic or a foreboding omen? You never knew in Gossip. Regardless, I had my suspect list and my starting point.

It was time to do what I did best. Poke the bear.

Later that morning...

With the clean up after the breakfast service complete, and a belly full of bacon and eggs, and Lauren's fantastic key lime pie, I took my grandmother's sea-green Mini-Cooper and headed off toward my first suspect's house.

Brenda Tippett. A local librarian.

Gamma had headed down to her secret armory below the Gossip Inn to do extra research on the suspects. Brenda was squeaky clean. Those had been my grandmother's exact words. Ones she hardly ever said when it came to folks in Gossip.

My grandmother was a firm believer that everybody had a secret, and Gamma happened to possess an iron will to discover what those secrets were.

Brewer Lane was a short street that ended in a cul-de-sac. Not the best place for a thief to live if they wanted to make a hasty escape.

I parked the Mini-Cooper and studied Brenda's gorgeous clapboard home. The front yard was neat, though the flowerbeds looked as if they were in need of watering, and the front door had been decorated with painted flowers.

The porch swing shifted in the brisk wind, and the screen door bumped against the frame occasionally.

I got out into the late morning warmth—a nice temperature since fall was finally on the way—and paused, lifting a hand to my forehead to shade my gaze from the sun.

Was it just me or was it awfully quiet this morning?

Sure, people had jobs to do and places to be, but the cul-de-sac was empty. Even Brenda's home seemed oddly silent.

My spy senses tingled.

I opened the cute picket gate and started up the path to the front porch. Yeah, the flowerbeds were super dry. Why hadn't they been watered? From the state of the house, it seemed like Brenda cared about her home, so why leave the flowers to wilt?

I made a mental note of it and jogged up the steps. I knocked on the front door, and it drifted open.

Uh oh. That's not good.

"Hello?" My voice echoed through the house. A long hall greeted me—polished wooden floors and cream walls holding picture frames. "Brenda? Are you home?"

No answer.

A tense silence hung in the interior.

"Miss Tippett?" Gamma's research had told me that Brenda lived alone. She was young and single, and had a lot of friends. Was it an invasion of privacy that my grandmother knew so much about everyone? Sure. But how else was an ex-spy meant to keep herself busy? Apart from building a kitten foster center-cat hotel combo.

"Miss Tippett?" I tried one last time before entering the house.

I walked down the hall, checking rooms left and right. First a living room, empty, but decorated in a homey style with floral covered armchairs and then an empty bathroom. I found the kitchen and stopped dead.

"Miss Tippett," I said, out of reflex.

Brenda Tippett lay on the kitchen floor, her cheek resting against the tiles, giving me a full view of her lifeless stare and the red flush of her cheeks. She had stretched out one arm, reaching toward the fridge. A chair lay beside her—the one she'd toppled out of.

Two items were on the kitchen table. A water bottle, uncapped, and a slice of key lime pie, a single bite taken from it.

Miss Tippett wasn't breathing. I didn't want to contaminate the scene, but just to be sure, I withdrew a pair of latex gloves from my purse and snapped them on, then pressed two fingers to Brenda's neck. No pulse.

Poisoning.

It had to be. Someone had fed Brenda Tippett a slice of poisoned key lime pie was my guess. This gave new meaning to the phrase "just desserts."

I backed out of the room, hastily removing my gloves, then got my phone out and dialled 911, walking back out to the porch, eyes peeled as I talked to the operator and described what I'd found. On the porch, I faltered, sucking in a breath.

There!

Several muddy boot prints had been left on the wooden boards in front of the porch swing, as if someone had vaulted over the railing instead of using the front steps. I put the call on hold to snap a picture of the prints.

Who had left them? And how? The garden was dry, the grass too, so where had the mud come from?

And why had my main suspect just been murdered?

❧ 6 ❧

"You're growing a track record for finding corpses." Detective Aaron Goode, as handsome as the first day I'd met him with his dark hair and sparkling green eyes, stood in front of me on the sidewalk. The police had already established a boundary—the yellow line was up across the front of the house. The coroner had arrived as well.

I bit down on the side of my tongue to keep from snapping at Detective Goode. He didn't need to know that he got under my skin. Or that finding this particular corpse had caused trouble for me.

I hadn't had the chance to find out if Brenda had stolen the recipe book. And, of course, it was terrible that she'd died.

Another mystery. This week is full of them.

"Earth to Charlotte," Detective Goode said, clicking his fingers. "You want to talk about what happened or should I call a therapist?"

"You know, Detective, you're so fun to talk to. I can't imagine why there are so many rumors about how rude you are spreading through town."

"People here have nothing better to do than talk," he said, unfazed by my jab.

"That's not true," I replied, nodding toward the house. "I think we've found a second passtime."

"And they say I'm fun." Detective Goode opened his notepad and clicked his ballpoint. "Well? What do you have to tell me?"

So many things you wouldn't like to hear. "Uh, are you questioning me?"

"Here I was thinking you had some level of social perception, Smith."

I balled up my fists. Man, this guy was as sassy as I was. Sassier, even, and it *bugged* me. He was like my Jessie Belle-Blue.

"Right, sure. It's just, I figured you'd want to ask questions that helped solve the crime rather than open-ended ones that'll get you nowhere."

"You leave the investigating to me, Miss Smith." He clicked his ballpoint another time. "Seriously. Leave it to me."

"Whatever." *And now I'm a teenager.* "Look," I said, "I came over to talk to Brenda Tippett about a recipe book this morning, and when I entered the house, I found her on the floor. In that state."

"Dead."

"Correct."

"And why did you enter the house?"

"I knocked and the door kind of drifted open," I said.

"Kind of or actually."

I rolled my eyes so hard that the center of my forehead hurt. "Figuratively. In the fourth dimension. As a tesseract."

"Hilarious."

"Ask dumb questions and you'll get the appropriate answers."

Detective Goode had gone red. Good. I was annoying him as much as he annoyed me. "So the door was open. What else did you see?"

"A dead woman. A set of muddy footprints on the porch near the swing." I gestured toward the house.

"Right. Tell me about this recipe book."

I didn't want to, but I was likely a suspect due to my presence at the house and the fact that I'd entered without Brenda's permission. "One of the guests at the Gossip Inn accused Brenda of having stolen her recipe book." I frowned. "Wait a second, you should know that. She reported that to you, didn't she?"

"And you thought it would be a good idea to come out here, and what, confront Miss Tippett about this allegedly stolen recipe book?" Goode ignored my question.

"Did Glendaree Bijon talk to you about the recipe book?" I countered.

"And what time did you leave the Gossip Inn this morning?"

"Around 10:30 a.m., but that's beside the point. Did Glendaree—?"

"I'll have to confirm your alibi with other witnesses," he said, flipping his notepad closed. "We might have a follow-up interview soon. Don't leave town." He walked off before I could repeat my question another time.

I considered yelling at his back. But, once again, it wouldn't do anything but annoy him and get me into trouble.

I had to let this go. For now.

7

I sat on the bench underneath our favorite tree in the inn's front yard. This was my rendezvous point with my grandmother—where we did most of our scheming, plotting and mission planning. We could be sure there was no one listening out here, and we could keep an eye on the front of the Gossip Inn while we were at it.

Gamma hadn't arrived for our "meeting" yet, so I waited, watching as birds swooped between the trees, the heat building the closer we got to the afternoon. The lunch service prep would start soon—I didn't have much time before I'd have to get to the kitchen and help out Lauren.

"Look alive, Charlotte," Gamma said, talking into my ear.

I managed not to jump. "Did you have to do that?"

"You're losing your edge," she replied. "We may not be in the 'business' any more, but we have to maintain a level of professionalism. One never knows when an old 'friend' might pay a visit."

Gamma was referring to the many enemies she'd gathered during her years as a spy. She had, so far, evaded attention. Nobody expected the most decorated spy in the NSIB's history to be hiding out in an inn in a tiny town in the middle of nowhere, Texas.

"Right," I said. "In my defense, I have been keeping fit."

"By fit, do you mean how many cupcakes you can fit into your mouth at once?"

"Sassy."

"Truthful," Gamma said, then rounded the bench and sat down. She patted me on the leg. "I'm just looking out for you."

My grandmother was rarely affectionate, and I smiled at her. "I know."

"So." Gamma smoothed her hands over her skirt, ensuring that it covered her knees appropriately. She was the picture of grace when she wasn't in black spy gear. "Tell me about Brenda Tippett's death."

News traveled fast in Gossip—I hadn't been explicit about why I'd wanted to rendezvous underneath the tree when I'd sent Gamma the text.

I told her everything I'd witnessed, and showed her the picture of the muddied boot prints that were at odds with the dry flowerbeds, recounted the kitchen's appearance, including the key lime pie and water, the state of the victim, and Brenda's red cheeks.

"Red cheeks, you say." Gamma tapped her chin. "A flushed face."

"Poisoning for sure."

"Remember the last time, Charlotte. One must learn from one's mistakes."

"I know, but this seems obvious. And I saw her corpse in full this time."

"Yes, I suppose you're right." Gamma fell silent, frowning.

"What?"

"Nothing. Nothing. I'll have to do some research on this," she replied. "It's interesting, that's all. What do you make of it, Charlotte? I'm intrigued to hear your opinion."

"I think I probably shouldn't get involved. I wasn't hired to solve a murder, but to find a recipe book," I replied. "But the temptation... Oh, man, you should've seen Goode's face when he arrived on the scene. He was enraged that I was there."

"Enraged?"

"Well, not enraged. He was doing that sarcastic, annoying—"

"Set aside your crush on the obnoxious detective for a moment, Charlotte."

"Crush!" I spluttered for a few seconds.

"Crush? You can't be serious, Georgina. Him? He's a— And me? I'm a— I wouldn't—"

"Stop. You're only making this worse for yourself."

I swallowed. "Anyway," I said, trying to ignore how hot my cheeks had grown. I'd been through enough with my ex-husband, and with my ex-boyfriend. I didn't need more man trouble. "Anyway, I should focus on the mystery of the recipe book."

"It might be that Brenda was murdered for the book. If it contained the winning recipe from last year, as Mrs. Bijon claims, there's motive. The baking competition does have a $5,000 grand prize."

"For baking a pie?"

"Apparently, it's a rigorous competition with several stages of elimination. They televize portions of it."

"We'll have to stay out of the way if that's the case."

Gamma nodded. "You have three suspects for the theft of the recipe book, and I'm already conducting research on them. But I believe you should add another name to the list."

I didn't have to ask whose. "Glendaree Bijon."

As if summoned from the nether by the mere mention of her name, the woman herself strode from the front of the inn, paused on the porch and lifted a hand to her forehead, shading her eyes as she scanned the inn's grounds.

She had changed out of her ridiculous bronze kaftan and opted for a silver one instead. Who knew wardrobe changes were a requirement when preparing for a baking competition?

"She might've taken her revenge on Brenda for stealing her recipe book," I said. "Or for allegedly stealing the recipe book. She's got a temper."

"Agreed."

Glendaree spotted us sitting under the tree—no rest for the wicked—and strode down the front steps, her kaftan whipping out

ROSIE A. POINT

behind her like a silvery tail. She strutted like she was on a catwalk, her glittery eye make-up practically blinding.

"You!" She stopped in front of us. "You were meant to be a professional!"

"Beg pardon?" Gamma arched an eyebrow at her.

"I'm talking to Miss Smith, not you," Mrs. Bijon snapped, turning on me again. "I hired you to do a job. To find the thief and my recipe book. Not go out to Tippett's house and discover her dead body."

"I went to interview a suspect you named," I replied, calmly. "She was dead. That's interesting, don't you think, Mrs. Bijon?"

"No, it's not interesting in the slightest, unless you're hiding my recipe book some-where underneath that disgusting outfit."

I had on a pair of plain blue jeans and a sleeveless blouse. "There's no need to get per-sonal, Mrs. Bijon. I'll find the thief and your recipe book. Rest assured." Interesting that she was so unconcerned about Brenda's death, though.

"You didn't even look around for the recipe book in her home, did you?" Mrs. Bijon replied.

"I found a corpse, Mrs. Bijon. A crime scene. I had no choice but to call the police. Where were you this morning?"

"I was at an appointment in town. And nevermind that! She might have been hiding the recipe book in her home! What if the police found it and took it in as evidence? What if I never get it back? I paid you the first half of your fee, Smith. I expect results."

"Quiet," Gamma said.

Mrs. Bijon opened her mouth and snapped it closed. Clearly stunned by the interruption and my grandmother's harsh tone.

"You won't speak to one of my staff in such a manner," Gamma said, then flicked her fingertips at Mrs. Bijon. "Go back to the inn and wait for your lunch. Now."

"How dare you. I will have you—"

"Now." Gamma gave her the icy stare that struck fear into the hearts of full-grown men. Criminals.

Mrs. Glendaree Bijon didn't stand a chance under that scrutiny. She tucked her silvery kaftan tail between her legs and hurried back toward the inn, not daring to look back.

"Annoying woman."

"She had a point," I said. "I need to get back to the crime scene. Poke around. See if I can find anything the police haven't. What if the recipe book was actually there and I missed it because I was doing the right thing?"

"You'll have to wait for them to release the scene," Gamma said. "You don't want to tamper with evidence."

I was irritated at the thought of Goode getting information I didn't have, but my grandmother was right. Disturbing a crime scene would get me in trouble and potentially expose my grandmother's position here in Gossip.

We had to be careful.

And I had to figure out who had stolen the recipe book. Besides, if I returned to Brenda's home, I might find a few clues that related to the murder. And if those just happened to fall into my lap, why shouldn't I use them to figure out who'd killed her? It would be doing Goode a favor, and keeping my favorite town in Texas safe.

❦ 8 ❦

The following day...

"Nothing," I said, adjusting my onion goggles on my face. "A big fat nothing." I cut into an onion, my vision hazy from the repurposed ski goggles and sniffled. My makeshift defense did a great job at preventing tears, but man, onions had one heck of a strong smell when cut. If I never cut another onion in my life, I would be satisfied.

"What's that, Charlie?" Lauren was in front of the stovetop working her magic for this afternoon's lunch service.

"There's been no new information about what happened to Brenda or the recipe book since yesterday. I can't find any of the suspects. It's like they've disappeared into thin air."

"Hmm?"

"Georgina's been helping me track the suspects," I explained. "Colton Harrison and Kayla Wren. We can't find either of them. Do you know where they are, perhaps?"

Lauren shrugged. "No, I'm sorry. I haven't heard much about either of them. I wish I could help, but I don't know *everybody* in town."

"Yeah, of course." Just because we lived in a small town didn't mean Lauren would know every person who'd been born in the local hospital. Gossip was small but it wasn't *that* small.

"I'm sure it will work out, Charlie. If anyone can help you find them, it's Georgina."

And she was right about that. I continued cutting onions, slicing them thick since Lauren wanted to make hamburgers with onion rings and fries.

I settled into the rhythm of working in the kitchen. It brought me joy simply because there was a routine to it, and routine had been a big part of my life for a long time when I'd been a spy. Doing things accurately and with purpose was my favorite part of, well, of life.

And trying to fix people's problems, whether it be finding stolen recipe books, clearing their names of a crime, or hunting down a murder, hardly ever wound up fitting the bill in that regard. It was difficult to be accurate when your suspects were MIA or refused to answer questions truthfully.

Gamma entered the kitchen, carrying a copy of *The Gossip Rag*.

"Uh oh," I said. "What is it this time?

More news about Belle-Blue's judging prowess and successful business skills?"

"I see the onions have worked their magic on your mood, Charlotte."

"Sorry," I grumbled. "I'm frustrated."

"We'll find the people you're looking for. I just need time. But for now, feast your eyes on this." She dropped the newspaper onto the table.

"My eyes are in famine mode at the moment." I pointed at the goggles. Luckily, I'd cut the last of the onions. I moved them over to the counter near the stove, then washed my hands, removed my onion goggles and joined my grandmother at the kitchen table.

Quinton McLarkal at large! Conviction overturned by appeals court!

And below that, a picture of a burly guy in an orange jumpsuit. He had a strong jawline and had a smiley face tattooed under one eye.

"Who is that?"

"Oh my heavens," Lauren gasped, nearly dropping her spatula. "I remember that case.

Are you serious? They overturned his conviction?"

"They have," Gamma said.

"Who is Quinton McLarkal?" I asked.

Gamma accepted a cup of coffee from Lauren before filling me in, her chin propped in her hand. "About four years ago, before you arrived in Gossip, we had a murder case that made headline news. Quinton McLarkal was accused of murdering a local man over a fish delivery. He was a fisherman, you see, and rumor had it that he was upset that the victim was moving in on his territory. It was an open and shut case, as far as the jury was concerned. He was sentenced to life in prison."

Lauren shivered. "I remember when it happened. Everyone was on edge. We're used to petty crime in Gossip, but murder? Horrible."

I bet that's changed. There've been quite a few murders since I arrived in town.

"Obviously, times have changed," Gamma said.

Lauren grimaced and started dipping the onion rings into batter.

"So what happened?"

"He appealed," Gamma said, "and it looks like the appeals court overturned the conviction. Apparently, one of the key witnesses lied and is being tried for perjury. And the case against Quinton fell apart."

"Did you know him well?" I asked.

"No," Gamma replied. "I didn't. I know a few minor details, but I never fleshed out my case file on the man since he was already imprisoned. What about you, Lauren?"

"Distantly. But I never talked to him. Honestly, I don't think anyone knew much about the guy. He was kind of a mystery."

"And he's out now?" I studied the picture.

"He's out. And probably returning to Gossip," Gamma said. "If he hasn't returned already."

"As long as he wasn't here before Monday..."

"That would be interesting to find out. But

I highly doubt the first thing a freed murderer will do is kill again." Gamma sighed. "Regardless, it's yet another strange turn of events in an entirely odd week."

I couldn't help but agree. But was Quinton's untimely release related to Brenda's murder? It was something to occupy my time while we searched for the other suspects.

I took the paper from my grandmother and read the article, but it didn't provide much information about when he'd been released and whether he would return. Of course, even Jacinta Redgrave, the editor of the local paper and gossiper in chief, couldn't predict that.

The released convict's eyes stared up at mine, blank, and I stared back, frowning.

Was it just me or did this man look awfully familiar?

9

Two days had passed since the discovery of Brenda's body, and the crime scene had finally been released. Rumor had it that a relative from out of town would soon arrive to take care of Brenda's affairs. Time was short. This was my opportunity to break into the house, search for the recipe book, and get out fast.

I checked my reflection in the mirror over my dressing table. I wore black pants, a black cardigan, and a pair of leather gloves. "What do you think?"

Cocoa Puff lay at the end of my bed, his two front paws tucked beneath his furry chest. He cracked an eye and let out a mini-meow.

"Do you think I should take my gun along? Just in case?" It wasn't a serious question. This was a recon mission. I wasn't about to attack somebody if they found me. I would be as silent as a shadow thanks to my grandmother's advanced spy gear.

I walked over to Cocoa, gave him a kiss on the furry forehead, then exited into the silent halls of the inn.

It was past midnight, and the guests were asleep. The perfect time had arrived for conducting illicit business, and I had a meeting with my favorite contact in the armory underneath the inn.

After two days of sheer irritation at the lack of leads in my case—I'd been unable to find and question either of the other suspects —I was finally on my feet again, moving toward a goal.

No way will I let Goode solve this before I do. A ridiculous thought.

I slipped out of the kitchen door and into the night. It was a new moon, the darkness complete apart from the distant glimmer of porch lights around the front of the inn. My feet crunched lightly on the gravel.

The doors to the basement were shut, but unlocked, the luminous mushrooms Lauren had painted on them bright despite the gloom. I bent to open the doors and a rustling in the bushes at my back stopped me.

I spun around but all was quiet.

Werewolf? Very funny, Charlie. Get real.

I descended into the basement quicker than usual and made for the armory door. Inside, my grandmother sat at her touchscreen desk at the front of the armory, dressed in black and already wearing her form-fitting armor—breathable fiber that deflected bullets and was easy to move in. Gamma had contacts in the spy world who owed her plenty of favors.

"Charlotte," she said. "I have good news."

"I could use some after the past couple of days." I smiled at the sight of the rows of shelves containing ammunition, and the three armor-bearing mannequins near the wall that contained a hidden compartment of weapons, legal and illegal.

I loved this place. It always put me in a good mood. There were plenty of hidden compartments containing high-tech gear too.

"Come take a look at this."

I joined Gamma at her state-of-the-art touchscreen desk. She tapped it and opened up an image of the first of the two suspects that had evaded us this week. "This," she said, "is Colton Harrison. He's one of the entrants for the baking competition and has spent the last week flitting around town collecting supplies. No one, and I mean none of my grapes on the vine, could tell me where he's been living for the past month. He's been moving around in town and out of it, a lot."

"Out of it?"

"Living on smallholdings, in trailer parks. It's odd," Gamma said. "Apparently, he's a paranoid individual. Usually works at the local coffee shop as a barista, but the owner cuts him a lot of slack because he has mental health issues. I contacted a friend who hacked some of the cameras in the businesses along Main Street and found this."

Gamma brought up a video feed on the screen, and a blurry image of a man matching Colton's height and hair color—blond— walked down the sidewalk, carrying a bag from a local boutique.

"Ah," I said. "You found him."

"I contacted the owner of the Butter-scotch Boutique, and she gave me his information. He's currently living in the Happy Camper trailer park just outside of town. I'll send the information to your mobile phone."

"You're amazing, Georgina."

"Pah." Gamma tried not to show her pleasure at the compliment and failed spectacularly. "And next on the list is Kayla Wren. She's not from Gossip but her family lives here. Interestingly enough, she's opted to stay at Belle-Blue's *establishment*. It took me a while to find her because none of Belle-Blue's women would talk to me. Idiots. But she's there."

"That presents a problem."

"Agreed," Gamma said. "But at least we know where they are."

"Anything on Glendaree or our victim, Brenda?"

"Yes, most definitely," Gamma replied. "Brenda Tippett is our local librarian, as you know."

The last time a librarian had died in Gossip we'd nearly gotten in trouble with the law. Hopefully, history wouldn't repeat itself.

"By all accounts, Brenda was a darling. Sweet to everyone she met. As I mentioned previously, unmarried, kept a lot of friends, that kind of thing."

"Right." Would a librarian steal a book? Even a recipe book?

"And then there's Bijon," my grandmother

said, her tone souring. "What a piece of work. The woman has a legacy of winning competitions, stepping on her friend's toes to get there, and giving interviews that are... quite frankly, a masterclass in how not to make friends."

"Dale Carnegie rolling in his grave?"

"Precisely." Gamma sighed. "But there's no criminal record."

"So, we don't have much on her."

"No, we don't. I can't confirm her alibi about an appointment without more information either, and she was unwilling to talk to me." Gamma raised a finger and tapped it on the screen, dulling it. "But after hours of research and deductive reasoning, I believe I've figured out the murder weapon."

Excitement built in my chest. "You have?"

"Poisoning by cyanide," Gamma said. "The flushed cheeks are a common symptom, and the fact that there was only one bite of key lime pie..."

"You think there was so much cyanide in the pie that it killed her instantly?"

"Actually, no," Gamma replied. "Here's the thing, a high dose of sugar can actually save someone from cyanide poisoning."

"Then, how?"

Gamma gave me a sneaky grin. "The bottle of water. She likely took a bite of the normal key lime pie, but the water was poisoned. Someone must've stopped by and given it to her. She had a lot of friends, so suspects abound, including those who might be after the recipe book."

"Which makes finding the recipe book even more important." Technically, that was my goal, even if I did not-so-secretly want to figure out who had killed Brenda.

"Exactly. But I can't confirm that it was cyanide poisoning for sure. Not without a sample of the water. Unlikely now as it's in police custody. We'll have to wait for them to release that information before we use it. We wouldn't want to follow a false lead." Gamma rose from her seat. "You'd better put on your armor just in case, Charlotte. Join me at the back of the room when you're done."

I did as I'd been told, ensuring that the body armor was firmly secure.

Gamma stood in front of one the glass boxes that populated the center and back of the armory, a grin parting her lips. This was her favorite part of our operations—impressing me with her gadgets.

"Tonight, I've prepared two special items for our entry into the Tippett house," she said, then tapped out a rhythm on the side of the box. A pneumatic hiss sounded and a pedestal rose from within, parting the glass and sliding into place in front of us.

Two plastic containers, identical in size, and small enough to fit in my palm, sat atop the pedestal.

"That's it? Our secret weapon this time is plastic?"

"These," Gamma said, lifting one of the containers and popping it open, "are night vision contact lenses. One set for you and for me. Pop them in. They adjust to the lack of light. We've used them before, remember?"

"Right, of course." We'd used them over a year ago to help bring down my rogue spy ex-husband.

"And the second item..." Gamma moved to a second glass box and tapped out another pattern. Again, a pneumatic hiss and the rising of the pedestal within. On this one sat what looked like a simple remote. "Remote scrambler. Disables house alarms from a distance and it can send out a small scale electromagnetic pulse that will shut down cellphones and electronics. Just in case we run into trouble." Gamma winked and handed it to me. "First button is the scrambler. The big red one is for the EMP. Try not to hit it accidentally. You'll fry your phone."

"I'll be leaving my phone at home then." I smiled at my grandmother. "Very impressive as usual."

"Indeed," she said. "We should take the SUV tonight to avoid attention."

"Meet you out front! I'm going to drop off my phone upstairs." I exited the armory, enjoying how green light filtered into my vision and clarified details the darker it became, and started up the steps to the basement doors.

A mournful howl rent the night. It had come from outside the inn! I burst from the basement, searching for the source of the noise, but was greeted by nothing but silence. The inn's grounds were crystal clear thanks to the night vision contact lenses, but there was nothing. No wolf. No... anything.

Then what had made the noise? It had to be a dog, right? But how had it gotten away so quickly? The howl had sounded close. Too close for comfort.

I set off around the side of the inn. There was no use worrying about supernatural creatures when there was a real "monster" hiding in Gossip. Brenda's murderer.

❧ 10 ❧

Gamma parked the SUV down the road from Brenda Tippett's house at 02:30 a.m.. "According to my research, it's around about this time when most people are in their deepest sleep. If we happen to cause a disturbance, it's less likely that we'll be seen."

"Good to know." I peered at the cul-de-sac. It was eerie how quiet the houses were, especially with a green haze over those that didn't have their porch lights on.

Why was I so spooked out lately? Maybe it

was Halloween on the horizon. Or it could be the impending ghost tours we were about to perform at the inn. Or Lauren's werewolf sighting.

I'd been desperate for some excitement, and now that I had it, I was anxious? No way. Not a chance.

"Charlotte," Gamma said, "we're going to do this cleanly. I know you're desperate to prove that you've still got it, but—"

"What? What's that supposed to mean?"

Gamma sniffed. "Come now, I raised you. I'm adept at reading your moods. You've been bored lately."

"Yeah, I freely admit that."

"But it's not really boredom that's bothering you. You're unsettled because you want to fit in and fix things."

"Spare me the professional empty nest syndrome talk. We already went down that road."

"Suit yourself," Gamma said. "But you're going to have to decide whether being a maid at the inn is what you *really* want. And soon."

"I do want to live at the Gossip Inn."

"That's not what I meant and you know it." But Gamma clapped her gloved hands before I could continue the argument. "Let's focus on what we have to do. Tell me about the crime scene in detail so that we know exactly what to expect."

I broke down exactly what I'd seen. We'd already gone over the layout of the house—a single story that wouldn't give us too much trouble to navigate.

"I took a picture of the footprints on the porch that I've already shared with you," I said, "but other than that, there's not much else."

"Right." Gamma nodded. "I've been trawling through the information I have, but I don't record information on shoes unfortunately. Another area of my database I'll be updating." She tapped her fingertips on the SUV's steering wheel. "We enter the home through a back door. You'll take the kitchen and living room. I'll take bedroom and bathroom."

"Copy that."

"Earpiece and microphone in place?" Gamma asked.

"Testing," I said, activating the flesh-colored patch pressed to my throat. "Are you reading me?"

Gamma touched her throat. "Loud and clear," she whispered, though her answer was loud in my ears. "On my count." She counted down from three on her fingers, and we slipped out of the car together, moving across the street in silence.

We vaulted over the picket fence and circled the house. The back windows were shut tight, colored green by my night vision lenses.

"Hit the button, Charlotte." Gamma in my earpiece.

I reached into my utility belt and hit the button on the scrambler. If Brenda had a house alarm, it was disabled now.

Gamma moved up the back steps of the house, removing a silvery tube from her pocket. She hit a button on the side and attached it to the back door's lock. A satisfying click rang out seconds later, and she opened the door.

We were in.

Now came the hard part. I followed my grandmother inside then proceeded to close the curtains in the kitchen. Gamma moved off, quietly, heading for the bedroom and bathroom to do the same.

Finally, I began my search. The night vision was a marvel, allowing me to move around and search for clues without needing any light and potentially alerting the neighbors.

"Anything?" I breathed, as I rooted through the kitchen cupboards for evidence.

"Nothing yet. No diaries or incriminating documents. And no recipe book."

I didn't reply, hiding my disappointment. But my search was as fruitless as my grandmother's. The living room, though it had a bookcase stocked with books, bore no sign of the recipe book.

I frowned, standing with my hands on my hips beside the coffee table.

There's got to be something here. Something...

I cast my mind back to the day of Brenda's murder and sucked in a breath. She had died on the floor with one hand out, stretching toward the fridge. Why the fridge? My initial thought was that she'd wanted water, but no, she'd had water right there on the table.

"I'm going to check out the fridge," I whispered.

"Now is hardly the time for a midnight snack, Charlotte."

The kitchen was quiet, and the inside of the fridge was empty apart from an old carton of milk and some orange juice. The magnets arranged on it didn't spell out a coded message from the dead woman, unfortunately.

Nothing on top of the fridge either. I lowered myself onto my knees, keenly aware that

I was now in a very similar position to the one in which I'd found Brenda.

There!

A slip of paper had fallen under the fridge. This must've been what Brenda had been trying to get at.

"I think I've found something," I said.

"On my way to you."

I got up, grabbed the sides of the fridge and walked it forward, swinging my weight from side-to-side.

"Heavens, Charlotte, are you trying to break your back?"

"There's something under the fridge." I stopped. "Unless you have a miniature forklift in your pocket?"

"I'll talk to my R and D guys about it."

"I'm going to assume you're joking," I replied, then walked around the side of the fridge and retrieved the now exposed slip of paper. I turned it over and read it. "Would you look at that? It's a 'thank you' note."

"From?"

"It doesn't say." I checked both sides of the paper then returned to stand next to my grandmother.

Thank you for your help with the recipe book. ;)
Hope you enjoy the pie.

"It's not signed," Gamma said. "Shoot."

"And it's a printed note," I put in. "Printed on a computer on standard paper so that whoever did this wouldn't get identified by their handwriting. Smart."

"And annoying." Gamma took the note with gloved hands, removed an evidence bag from her pocket, and slipped the piece of paper into it. "We'll need to keep this for when you find the murderer, Charlotte. You can hand it over to Detective Goode then."

Because, now I had no choice. The note had connected my client's missing recipe book with the murder.

If we found the murderer, we found the book.

❧ II ❧

Early the next morning...

I yawned my way into the kitchen, my mind swimming with theories that were implausible, improbable or a mixture of both. Either way, I needed to figure out who had left Brenda the incriminating note and how they had gotten hold of Mrs. Bijon's recipe book.

The evidence so far seemed to indicate

that Brenda had indeed had the book and had passed it on. But to whom? That was the case-solving question.

"Good morning, Charlie," Lauren said, from the counter. She smiled and paged through her sacred recipe book—what was it with chefs and their recipes?

"Hey, Laur. How are you feeling?"

"Well," she said, huffing. "I'm five days away from my due date and Jason is trying to ban me from taking part in the Tri-State Baking Competition this weekend, but other than that, I'm heavy, sore all over, and the baby keeps doing this thing where he stretches out pokes me in the ribs and the bladder at the same time."

"Remind me never to get pregnant."

"Apart from that, Jason also has another meeting this month and he's complaining about having to cancel it because money's hardly flush at the moment. I mean, Georgina pays me well, but with a family of four and his business slower than usual, it hasn't been easy.

You have no idea what it's like to have a nag-ging, whining husband."

"And I'll add 'never getting married' to the reminder list."

Lauren flipped another page in her recipe book without looking at me. "And on top of that, Tyson's started going to daycare and the teacher says he bit a kid."

"Does Tyson even have that many teeth?"

"He's got the bottom and the top, and the others are pushing through, so I guess you could say he gummed the kid?"

"What did he do?" I asked.

"I imagine he picked up the boy's finger and, you know." She mimed snapping her teeth shut.

"No, I mean, the other kid. Tyson's a cutie. He wouldn't hurt a fly. If he bit the kid, I'm sure there's a good reason for it."

"Oh my." Lauren let out a peal of laughter. "That's not how that works, Charlie. Kids can't just go around biting other kids. That's a recipe for tetanus."

"I assume that's not one of the recipes in your book?"

"Hilarious." But Lauren didn't say it in that grumpy, "Shut up, I'm pregnant" way. She spared me a smile. "I'm happy you're around, Charlie. You always brighten my morning. But you look like somebody dragged you out of bed backward."

"That would be Sunlight. He had a case of the zoomies last night."

My special orange kitty meowed at me from the hall where he sat outside the kitchen's archway. The cats were not allowed into the kitchen under any circumstances and both Cocoa and Sunlight played by the rules.

The other cats, the ones in the kitten foster center down the hall, never entered this section of the inn anyway.

"Oh," Lauren said, "I thought maybe that werewolf kept you up. But, of course, how silly of me. Werewolves can't change if there's no full moon."

"Yeah. That's the silly part. So, where do you need me?" *Please not onions. Please not onions!*

"I want to make banana cupcakes," Lauren said. "So you can start by slicing some bananas."

"Perfect." I could slice bananas while I sat at the kitchen table and sipped coffee. I prepared everything and sat down. I worked methodically, placing the neatly sliced bananas in a bowl to one side.

The case played on my mind.

Brenda had handed off the recipe book to the person who had killed her. Unless, the recipe book mentioned in the note wasn't actually the same as the one that had been stolen from Mrs. Bijon. But what were the chances of that?

And then there was the newly released murderer to think about. Surely, he had nothing to do with this.

"—talking about how Brenda's boyfriend might be the one. I think that's quite distasteful but what can you do? People in this town love to gossip and—"

"Wait a second," I said. "What did you just say?" Lauren had a habit of talking nonstop in the mornings and since I was usually exhausted and not a morning person I'd gotten into the opposite habit of tuning her out.

"About what? The gossiping? It's sinful but what can you do? There's not much else to keep a woman entertained in this town. Or a man. Mr. Eldoy at the hardware store is just as much of a gossip as any woman in this town, if you ask me. But of course, don't tell him I said that."

"No, not about that. About Brenda's boyfriend?"

"Oh, that? There have been a few rumors about him," Lauren said. "Unpleasant ones."

"Such as?"

"That he was the last person who saw poor Brenda alive. You see, he lives right next door to her so they go running together before she goes to the library. And Natalie at the silverware store said that Misty Primrose overheard them arguing the night before Brenda, you know." Lauren pulled a face. "You see, Misty Primrose lives on the other side of Brenda and she's always home."

"She is?"

"Yeah, she's one of those freelance graphic designers. She's always working from home. She needs a good internet connection and loads of coffee and that's about it," Lauren continued. "I mean, it's amazing what people can do nowadays with so little."

"Yeah."

"And Misty's always been on the shy side too, you know. In high school, she was the outsider. Preferred to sort of, sit around and watch people rather than interact. Socially awkward. Poor girl. And now, she's saddled with her mother's mortgage and there's that whole issue with the dogs down the street, I can barely imagine how she copes. A working class hero."

"John Lennon would be proud?"

"Who?"

I stared at her, blinking repeatedly. "Tell me you're joking."

"I never kid about death, Charlie," Lauren said. "There are two things that are certain in life. Death and that there is no greater pain than childbirth while your husband snaps unflattering pictures of your nether region."

I put up a hand. "We're getting off-track," I said. "You mentioned that the boyfriend might've been the last person to see Brenda alive?" My fatigue had dropped away at the prospect of a new lead.

And the fact that the boyfriend lived in the same street as Brenda made this even better. Even if he hadn't done it—the note about the recipe book had to *mean something*—he might've heard or seen something. The neighbors too.

"Yeah. That's what Misty says, anyway. You should talk to her if you want to find out more. She lives on Brewer Lane too. I can give you the address and her cellphone number."

"Thanks, Lauren."

"Careful with those banana slices, Charlie. You don't want to make them too chunky."

I returned my focus to the breakfast prep, tamping down on my excitement. It was time to get sleuthing.

❧ 12 ❧

I parked my grandmother's Mini-Cooper at the entrance of the cul-de-sac, beside a house with tall green hedges bordering it, and took quick stock of the scene.

To the left of Brenda's quaint, clapboard home was a nearly identical one, the only difference being the door was unpainted, and the guy in the front yard. He walked around with a shovel, wearing a pair of gardening gloves, and stopped to dig in the flowerbeds.

The boyfriend. Lauren had given me the

addresses and numbers for both Misty and the boyfriend, and this was the correct address. Not that it took rocket science to figure out what "he lives next door to Brenda" meant.

I emerged from the car and strolled over, tucking my hands into the pockets of my jeans. "Hi," I called, noting that it was pretty darn weird how Brenda's boyfriend had decided to do gardening work so soon after she'd died.

The muddy prints?

I glanced down at his shoes, but he wasn't wearing any. The man stood barefoot, dirty toenails and all, in the flowerbed. He stopped digging the shovel into the ground and rested a forearm on its handle, wiping sweat from his forehead with the back of his hand.

"Who are you? You don't live around here."

Who shall I be today?

In my experience, suspects didn't often like talking about crimes, and I would get in trouble with Detective Goode if I messed this up.

"I'm sorry to interrupt you," I said, "but are you Norman Sweet?"

"Yeah," he replied. "That's right. Who are you?"

"My name is Carly Jones." I stuck out a hand, grinning at him. "I'm from *Gossip News Online*. We're an upcoming online publication aimed at delivering the people of Gossip the news, more news, and nothing but the news. Haha!" I completed the sentence with a suitably goofy chuckle.

My favorite part of being a spy had been incapacitating people and the least favorite playing a role, but I was desperate.

Norman wiped his sweaty hand on his blue jeans and accepted my shake. It was as damp as I'd expected it to be. "Nice to meet you," he said, then glanced at Brenda's house.

I took that moment to study his features. Sharp nose, and dark eyes, tan skin, and a receding hairline, but not unattractive. Early thirties, maybe? And Brenda had been around a similar age so that added up.

"You here to talk to me about... about Brenda?"

"Yes," I said, "if that's all right with you."

His brow furrowed.

"You see," I continued, before he could say anything I would regret, "we at *Gossip Online* want to ensure that the truth is told about current events."

"Wait a second, didn't you say you were from *Gossip News Online?*"

"Yeah, that's what I said. *Gossip News Online.*" Of course, I'd messed up that part already. "So, about those nasty rumors, Mr. Sweet."

"What rumors?" He stiffened out of leaning on the end of his shovel. It flopped over and hit the picket fence with a bonk. "Who's been spreading rumors about me?"

"Well, everybody, Mr. Sweet. Haha!" *Was*

that goofy laugh too much? Maybe I need to dial it back a bit. "Everybody's saying that *you* were the last one to see Brenda alive. And you know what that means, don't you?"

His expression darkened. "Now, you listen here—"

"I just wanted to make sure that you had a chance to say your piece. To set the record straight."

"There's no record! No straightening required. I told everything I know to the cops."

I was losing him. Shoot. *Come on, Charlie.* "You're probably right. It doesn't matter that everyone thinks you murdered your girlfriend in cold blood." I turned to walk away.

"Now, you wait one hot second!" The gate clacked. Norman caught up to me. "Just wait. Listen. Listen for a second."

I turned to him. "Yes?"

"I didn't do anything to Brenda. Heck, I didn't even see her on the morning she died. I had to leave early for work, you see? And

Brenda was tired because she stayed up late baking pies and meeting with her friends."

No mention of their alleged argument. "Which friends?"

"I don't know. She doesn't tell me her every move. I mean, she didn't. She never used to... aw, nevermind." He exhaled. "I didn't see Brenda that morning. I didn't see anything except..."

"Except?"

"There was this white car that circled the block," he replied. "It was weird. It was early in the morning so the streets are usually quiet. I didn't expect to see anyone around, but this white car, I think it was a hatchback, Kia thing, I didn't pay much attention, circled the block then drove off. That's it. I bet whoever was in that car did it."

"You do?"

"Sure." Norman Sweet gulped. "Just make sure you put that in your online article thing. That I saw a white car. And that I wasn't here. That's it. OK?"

"Thank you, Mr. Sweet."

But as I watched him skedaddle, barefoot, back into his garden, I couldn't help noticing how easy it would've been for him to jump over the fence in muddy boots and stride up to Brenda's front door.

13

"Lauren told me you would come by." Misty poked her head around the corner of her door, but didn't invite me into her home.

When Lauren had told me the woman who lived on the other side of Brenda's home was shy, she hadn't been kidding.

"Oh, good," I said. "I'm sorry to interrupt you like this but I wanted to ask a couple of questions about what happened to Brenda Tippett."

"Yeah, I get that. I'm always home, and I'm always keeping an eye on the neighborhood. You know, I talked to that handsome detective too." Misty brushed red hair away from her pale cheeks. "He's kind of cute, don't you think?"

Had Lauren put her up to this? No, Lauren didn't know that I... ahem, despised Detective Goode and his arrogant behavior. "So, I talked to Brenda's boyfriend."

"Oh, Norman?" Misty's voice was timid and slightly squeaky. She reminded me of a mouse inching toward cheese in a trap. "Yes, so, Norman was supposedly the last one who saw her alive. And I heard them arguing the night before. But yeah, last one to see her alive."

"Do you think that's true?"

"I can't say," she replied, unhelpfully. "Norman leaves for work pretty early most days, I know because I was pulling an all-nighter for a client once and I saw him leaving at around 04:00 a.m. so... yeah."

"And that wasn't on the morning of Brenda's murder?"

Misty paled and let out a little squeak, her fingers tightening on her door. "No, that wasn't then. No. No, you see, on the morning of Brenda's... on the day.. on *that* day... you know, the day it—"

"It happened?" I suggested.

"Oh yes, on the day it happened," she said, relieved at finding an appropriate euphemism, "I woke up at about 08:30 a.m. which is well after Norman leaves for the morning."

"And did you see Brenda at all?"

"No, no, not at all. No," Misty breathed. "I noticed that her house was quiet. You see, she's been having a lot of guests over lately. She started a baking club out of her house. I think it's because there's this big baking competition that's going to happen soon."

"Right," I said. "And did you see anyone going into Brenda's house?"

"No, no, not at all. No," she said. "But it wasn't as if I was looking out for her. I might've missed someone visiting or even Brenda leaving. I usually keep my curtains closed. I don't like a lot of light when I'm working on a project. I find sensory deprivation is great for the creative process."

I wasn't about to dispute that. I had about as much creativity as a pickle. "Did you see anything strange that day?"

"Let me think. I noticed a car driving down the street that was unfamiliar. It was white. I think it was... I'm not good with cars, but I think it was a Kia? I didn't see who was driving it though, and it might not have been related to Brenda's death."

So, that was twice that a white car had been seen, by both the boyfriend and Misty.

"Was there anything else that seemed unusual to you?" I asked.

"Only the new—"

A slam sounded from Brenda's house, and Misty let out a horrified squeak and shut the door in my face.

"Misty?" I knocked. "Hello, Misty?"

"Who's making that noise?" The voice came from Brenda's front yard. A woman stood there with brown hair. She was in her late thirties, and wore a pair of thick glasses and a strappy white dress that cut into her skin.

"Hi," I said. "Sorry. That was me."

"Oh. Well, try to keep it down. Some of us are trying to work over here." The woman headed for Brenda's front door, mail in hand.

"Wait!" I called after her, rushing down the steps and toward the line of fence that separated Misty's property from Brenda's. "Wait a second."

"Yeah?" The woman clomped back down to meet me. She stopped short of the dry flowerbeds.

"Are you... sorry, I don't mean to pry, but are you related to the woman who passed?"

"Yes," she said. "I'm Marie. Brenda's sister." She shook my hand, her grip clawlike and her nails manicured.

A white dress for a woman in mourning?

"I'm sorry for your loss," I said. "This must be difficult for you and your family."

"Family? Sheesh, there's no family left except for me." Marie grinned. "I'm the last person Brenda had."

"As I understand it, she had a lot of friends." Why didn't Marie know that about her sister?

"Fairweather friends, you mean. I'm sure they wouldn't have given two hoots about her if she went through troubled times. Anyways, trust Brenda to go and get herself killed." Marie clicked her tongue. "She was always leaning on me, and she's left me just about everything to do. Did you know even her alarm was broken? Like... I'm the one who has to deal with that now. Unbelievable."

"I'm sorry about that." Not really. Marie was giving me sinister vibes.

"Ah, that's fine. I work in the city. I'm used to dealing with big messes like this. Always used to tell Brenda that this tiny town would be the death of her, but she never listened.

She was so stubborn. That's one thing I won't miss about her." She guffawed. "But I'll miss the other stuff." She said that last part quickly, like she realized her behavior wasn't normal for a grieving family member. "I'd better get back to it." She gestured up to the house.

"Sure," I said. "But hey, Marie?"

"Yeah?" She stopped halfway across the yard, looking back over her shoulder at me.

"Do you have any suspicions about who might've done it?"

"Oh yeah. You ask me, it was that boyfriend of hers. I lost count of the amount of times she called me upset about a fight they'd had. Poor girl." And then she headed inside, the screen door slamming shut behind her.

The vernacular was all wrong. The behavior equally so. The white dress? Something was off about Marie Tippett. She was officially on my suspect list.

🜲 14 🜲

I got into my grandmother's Mini-Cooper, my mind on my next target.

Kayla Wren. The soft-spoken baking competitor who Mrs. Bijon had listed as a prime suspect for stealing the recipe book.

I had about an hour before I needed to be back at the Gossip Inn to help prepare everything for lunch, and with Lauren in a whirl about the baking competition later this week, she needed all the support she could get.

But the short drive to the other side of

town helped me mull over the problem at hand.

Being that Kayla Wren was staying in Jessie Belle-Blue's guesthouse. I highly doubted my grandmother's arch enemy would allow me to waltz in and start questioning her guests.

Twenty minutes later, I stepped out into the late morning sunlight, Jessie's guesthouse and combined cattery ahead of me.

How on earth am I going to do this?

If I'd had the opportunity, I'd break in, detain Miss Wren, and bring her back to the Gossip Inn for interrogation. But that was about as likely as Jessie Belle-Blue growing a conscience and apologizing for her constant slights against Gamma.

I stopped on the sidewalk outside the gate, fisting my hips.

The front door of the guesthouse crashed open before I'd finished considering the horrible turn of events that had brought me to Jessie Belle-Blue's doorstep.

The pashmina queen herself stormed onto the porch. "No!" she cried, with a flick of the ends of her lace-frilled pashmina. "Absolutely not."

"Eh?"

"Do you think I'm stupid?" Jessie strode down the pathway that led from her witchy-looking home to the front gate. Her eyes were a striking blue, her auburn hair—straight from a bottle—styled in a bob, and her stubby legs ensconced in velvet.

"Good morning, Miss Belle-Blue," I said.

"It's Mrs. Brown to you!"

Be that as it may, Jessie would remain "Belle-Blue" to me. The evil ring of the name had lodged itself in my brain.

"Get off my property," Belle-Blue snapped, before I could tell her the reason for my presence.

"I'm on the sidewalk. Technically, that's public property. Look, I didn't come to get into an argument or upset you, I just wanted to—"

"That idiot, Georgina, has sent you to spy on me. Don't even try to deny it. I won't allow your presence here. If you don't leave, I'll call the police."

"Jessie, come on," I said, trying for a soft smile, one that Charlotte the maid would have used to de-escalate the tension. "I'm not even here to talk to you or to stay at your guesthouse." The guesthouse that had once been just a cattery and, before that, Jessie's home. "I want to talk to one of your guests."

"Get off my property!" Jessie roared.

I considered bopping her on the nose, but I wasn't going to get anywhere here. I retreated to Gamma's car. Jessie glared at me for a moment longer before retreating to the steps of the higgledy-piggledy guesthouse.

Futile.

I'd have to find out about Kayla another way. That left two names on my suspect list, Glendaree Bijon and Colton Harrison. I'd deal with Colton first, since he lived in the Happy Campers trailer park outside of town, and I hadn't had the opportunity to talk to him yet. And of course, I'd have to find out when Marie Tippett had arrived in town.

I put on my seatbelt, started the engine and—

My phone trilled in my purse. I fished it out to find my grandmother's number flashing on the screen.

"Georgina?"

"Come back to the inn, right away!" My grandmother's British accent was particularly pronounced when she was angry or excited. "There's been a development."

🐾 15 🐾

"I knew these cameras would be worth their weight in gold," Gamma said, the minute I entered the kitchen in the inn.

Lauren stood at the stove, stirring a pot of something fragrant and, I had no doubt, delicious. "It's a shock, Georgina. Are you sure about this?"

"Absolutely positive," Gamma said. "I'd know that silhouette anywhere."

"What are you going to do about it?" Lauren chewed her lip. "Oh, Georgina, it's just that the local contestants, the ones from Gossip, have arranged a private meet-up at the Hungry Steer and I'd hate for it to be ruined by this new... uh, development."

"Don't you worry about that, Lauren," Gamma said, raising her chin. "This information will go no further than you, me, and Charlotte."

"Somebody want to tell me what's going on?" I asked.

"Right. Yes. Of course. Wait here, Charlotte." Gamma hurried from the room, leaving behind the scent of her light, lemony perfume.

I sat down at the kitchen table. "What's for lunch today, Lauren?"

"I'm going to keep things simple," she replied. "And we're going to do double prep since I have that dinner meeting at the Hungry Steer. Corn chowder, hearty and delicious since today is cooler than usual, and then for dinner we'll do a simple pasta bake with crusty bread from The Bread Factory."

"Right. You have a dinner date," I said. "Just for local contestants, you said?"

"Yes. Us Gossipers have to stick together, you know. With the Tri-State Baking Competition drawing in so many outside entrants, and with that grand prize, there's bound to be people who want to cheat their way to the top. As much as I hate to say it." She grimaced. "I try to think the best of everybody, Charlie, but you can't deny that there are certain types who—"

"Mind if I accompany you this evening?" I asked, an idea occurring to me. Most of my suspects in the case were Gossip residents and baking competitors. This meeting sounded like the perfect opportunity to meet a few of them. Discover what they thought of Brenda's death.

"Sure. I guess. It's meant to be just for us contestants, but I'm sure it will be fine."

"It might give me a lead on the missing recipe book," I said.

"Oh right! Good idea. Then, why sure you can come, Charlie."

Gamma bustled into the kitchen, carrying her laptop. She opened a video feed on the screen. "This," she said, "is the footage from the side of the inn. It was taken late last night."

"What did they capture?"

"Wait and see."

I watched the screen, tension banding in my chest. If Gamma had called me back from my recon, it had to be important.

The shot was of the inn's grounds, the greenhouse and distant trees that led toward the creek bordering the property. It was a view from the camera seated along the kitchen's side of the inn.

"Watch this," Gamma said, shifting in her seat.

In the distance, near the greenhouse, a figure walked into shot. The person was hunched over, wearing what looked like a giant poncho or a... no! It was a pashmina.

And though the image wasn't exactly clear, I recognized the bob.

"Belle-Blue!" I whispered. "What on earth is she doing?" The time stamp in the bottom left corner of the screen put the footage at 03:00 a.m..

Gamma shook her head.

Jessie hovered near the greenhouse for a second before wandering into the trees. She didn't reappear.

"I knew she was up to something," Gamma hissed. "This has got something to do with her judging the baking competition. I'm sure of it!"

"She might be spying on the inn. Trying to gather information."

"Yes, of course, but she's never done this before and she's had ample opportunity. Why now? Why when she's been announced as a judge of the competition? What is she after? Something doesn't add up. I bet she was the one who murdered Brenda."

"Georgina," I said. "Let's be serious."

"I'm being serious." But my grandmother didn't add anything to the statement. Perhaps she realized that she'd gone too far.

While I'd love to help Gamma dig up dirt on her competitor, I didn't see that it would be conducive to my investigation. Glendaree Bijon had paid me to do a job. And I had committed myself to finding Brenda's murderer.

If only because I wanted to keep Gossip violence-free.

And what then? What happens when it's deathly quiet for the next few months? What are you going to do with your life? Be a fake maid? Live in the inn?

Those were questions I was *not* ready nor willing to answer.

"Say, Georgina," Lauren said, blowing on a spoonful of her chowder before taking a sip. "More salt. Say, Georgina."

"Yes?"

"Did you check the footage from your camera on the night I saw the werewolf?"

Gamma and I shared a look.

"No. It hadn't occurred to me." Gamma clicked a few times on the laptop's mouse pad. "But while we're here, why not?"

"Great!" Lauren left her chowder to bubble and came over to join us, bracing either hand on the backs of our chairs. "You'll see I was telling the truth. A werewolf. We'll have to find a way to get rid of it, you know."

I held back a sigh. Hopefully, the footage would show Lauren that she'd either imagined it or mistaken something innocuous for this "werewolf" she claimed to have seen.

Gamma brought up the footage from the other night, at around the time Lauren had arrived, also 03:00 a.m., oddly enough.

"There I am!" Lauren tapped my shoulder. "See?"

And indeed, the heavily pregnant chef waddled into view below the camera. Lauren froze on the bottom step, her eyes widening. She spun on the spot, turning to stare into the darkness, then threw up her hands.

"That's when I screamed the first time. And there, see! There's the wolf."

Gamma and I both leaned in, squinting at the screen.

I gasped. "Well, I'll be a donut's hole."

"Charlotte, that's verging on inappropriate."

"Sorry. I meant a cake's slice?"

"Better."

Under the trees, removed from the greenhouse in the inn's grounds, lurked a large, hulking shape with glowing eyes. It took a single step forward, exposing a long gray snout, a massive paw. Onscreen Lauren turned and dashed up the kitchen steps, she fiddled with the door, frantically.

"That's when I screamed the second time."

The kitchen door opened, and the chef disappeared inside. The shape, the, well, it was a wolf-like shape, to be fair, retreated into the darkness again.

"That's... OK." There had to be a rational explanation for this. Werewolves didn't exist.

"Interesting," Gamma said. "A coyote, perhaps?"

"No! No way," Lauren said. "I've seen one of those before and this wasn't it. Rewind the footage, please, Georgina. See? Look there. The coloring is wrong."

"Then what is it?" I asked my grandmother.

"I'm not sure. Some type of wild dog, perhaps?"

"Y'all are trying to be difficult." Lauren walked back to her chowder, brushing her fingers over her pregnant belly, an air of triumph about her. "It's a werewolf. Plain and simple."

❧ 16 ❧

That evening...

"I don't agree with this course of action, Georgina," I said, my phone pressed to my ear. "It feels like a bad idea. If you're suspicious of Jessie, you can go to the police. Show them the footage of her creeping around on your property."

"Let me handle this."

"I know you can handle it," I whispered,

standing beside Lauren's car. "That's not the problem. It's Belle-Blue that you can't handle. She drives you crazy and I don't want you to jeopardize—"

"I've got to run, Charlotte. This is important." And then she hung up.

My grandmother had decided that, while Lauren and I attended the meeting of the local baking competitors at the Hungry Steer, she would take on a reconnaissance mission of her own. At Belle-Blue's guesthouse. While she was a fantastic spy, I was always concerned when it came to my grandmother's dealings with Jessie.

"Charlie?" Lauren beckoned from where she waited at the front of the Hungry Steer. "Are you coming? I'm hungry enough to eat a steer."

We entered the Hungry Steer restaurant, run by the infamously oily tycoon, Grayson Tombs, and found our reserved booth at the back of the dining area. The interior was filled with hay bales, lanterns, and comfy red-backed chairs.

Three people awaited us in the booth.

First, a young woman with mousy brown hair, eyes darting left and right as she studied the others at the table. Kayla Wren. I'd seen her picture on my grandmother's touchscreen desk in the armory.

Second, the ever-illusive Colton Harrison, tall and weedy, with a weak chin and a wispy blond goatee, sat beside her, scrolling on his phone. He was in his early thirties by my guess.

And finally, a woman I didn't recognize—several extra chins, bearing a bright smile and wearing all pink. "Well, hello," she cried, fluffing her bright orange hair. "Nice to meet you both. You must be Lauren, yes? My sister told me about those lovely creations of yours at the Gossip Inn. I've been meaning to come by and meet you. Oh, forgive my rudeness. Deidre Hardecki." She extended a hand and shook Lauren's then mine. "And who are you? Another competitor?"

"I'm tagging along for moral support," I said, smiling at her. "Charlotte."

"Nice to meet you," Deirdre said. "Scooch down, y'all. Make space for the newcomers."

Kayla immediately shifted down. Colton took a second, offering us each a distracted glance before moving.

I slid in first so that Lauren could sit on the edge in case she needed to make a quick exit to use the ladies' room.

"Have you ordered yet?" I asked.

"Not yet. We were waiting for you." That had come from the soft-spoken Kayla, her eyelashes all aflutter. I didn't buy the act.

Deirdre waved at a server, and I cleared my throat. "So, you're entrants in the competition?" I said it, easily, hoping to spark a conversation.

The others merely nodded. Nothing. And I couldn't ask why Kayla was staying at Jessie's guesthouse without sparking questions as to how I knew that information.

"That's cool."

An awkward silence, broken only by the country music from the speakers, ensued until after the server, overly friendly to make up for the lack of smiles at the table, took our drinks and food orders. I'd gone for a hamburger and fries with a chocolate milkshake.

"I can't tell y'all how I excited I am for this contest," Deirdre started. "I just know I'm in with a good chance after hearing what some of the out-of-towners are preparing."

"Oh yeah?" Colton lifted his head, meeting her gaze. His demeanor was sharp and snappy. Straight to the point. "What did you hear?"

"Why ask me? It's Kayla who's found that information out for us." Deirdre winked at my mousy suspect. "Isn't that right, Kayla, darlin'?'

The younger woman blushed. "Well, I—it wasn't intentional. People tend to tell me things, that's all." She was barely audible.

"Speak up, honey," Deirdre blustered. "You're as quiet as a fart in church."

Colton grimaced at her. "Do you have to be gross?"

"It's a saying." Deirdre waved away his issue. "Get used to it, Colton dear, that's just how I talk."

"Like a trucker?"

"Kayla," I said, before things got too intense, "you were saying something about the contestants? Their entries?"

"What did you find out?" Lauren asked, politely.

"Yeah. Spill it." Colton glared at the girl. I couldn't help thinking of her as a girl, though she was surely in her mid-twenties.

Kayla worried her bottom lip. "Just that most of them want to make selections of donuts and lemon meringue pie. And then there are some who want to copy the idea of last year's winning entry."

"Bijon's key lime pie," Deirdre said, tapping her chin with a long, pink fingernail.

"How did you find this out?" I asked.

"I'm staying at a local guesthouse with some of the other contestants." She colored at the scrutiny from everyone at the table. "I... yeah."

"Why aren't you staying with your daddy?" Lauren asked.

Kayla's coloring turned a deeper red. "He's got business to attend to. He—"

"They want to make Bijon's pie, you said?" Colton talked over her. "What a dumb idea. Who would think that making the same pie two years in a row would work? The judges want something new. Fresh."

"Ain't nothing fresh about Bijon's pie," Deirdre agreed. "But did you hear about what happened?"

Everyone stared at her, expectantly.

The server arrived with our drinks, and Deirdre smiled at the tension-building interruption. It seemed Miss Hardecki enjoyed attention.

Once the server had withdrawn, she

waited a few moments before continuing. "As I was saying before we were so rudely interrupted," Deirdre continued, taking a sip of her drink, "Glendaree Bijon's recipe book was stolen a few days ago, and I'd bet anything that it was one of those out-of-towners who took it." She paused for effect. "Took it from Brenda Tippett's cold, dead body."

Kayla let out a shuddering gasp.

Colton groaned at the drama.

"Oh come on," Deirdre said. "You've heard the rumors, haven't you? Brenda was found in her house, stabbed through the heart, with a note written on the walls in her own blood."

"That's revolting," Colton said. "Don't talk about the deceased like that."

"Can you think of a worse way to be murdered?" Deirdre blustered on. "Murdered for a recipe book. They say that bad deeds beget bad deeds, and I hate to say it but Brenda had it coming. She took the recipe book from Bijon, hoping to win the contest, and then she got what she deserved."

"There's no proof of that," Kayla murmured. "Of any of that. Why do we have to talk about this at dinner? It's horrible."

"Yeah, death isn't exactly polite conversation."

"Well, gosh, gee, excuse me for trying to talk about something interesting," Deirdre replied. "Y'all are as quiet as—"

"Don't." Colton raised a hand. "Brenda's murder and the recipe book have nothing to do with us."

"Sure. But they have everything to do with the competition. I figure that either it was one of these jealous out-of-towners who got her or it was Bijon herself," Deirdre continued. "She found out that Brenda took the book and decided to get her revenge. What do you make of that?"

No one answered her.

Deirdre sucked down some pop then rolled her eyes, grumbling under her breath. The conversation went quiet for a while before Lauren picked it up by talking about who would be baking what, and how nervous they all were.

And I was left wondering why I had decided to tag along in the first place. My discoveries didn't exactly shed light on the case. Kayla had a father who was ill and lived somewhere in town, though she hadn't given a reason for staying at Jessie's guesthouse, and Colton was a brash, no-nonsense man.

That was all.

Sheesh, maybe I should've gone on the reconnaissance mission with Gamma after all.

17

"Now, I'm so glad to have met y'all." Deirdre hadn't quit talking since we'd risen from the dining table. She'd followed behind us into the parking lot, right up to Lauren's car. "And by that I mean, just you two. Those others are so dry my skin started turning ashy."

"It was nice to meet you too, Deirdre," Lauren said, sweetly.

"Yeah." That was as far as I could take it without exposing myself.

Lauren unlocked her car door and opened

it, placing one foot inside while Deirdre continued talking.

"You know, it's so nice to meet people who actually care about baking. And gossip too." She winked. "I can't stand people who think they're better than others. You know, like that Colton. Acting like he's all high and mighty when we all know he's got about three different jobs, and he lives in the trailer park."

Lauren opened her mouth to say something.

"And don't even get me started on that Kayla girl. Mild as milk and with hardly two pennies to rub together. You heard about her father, I assume? Being ill? As if. The man's never been ill a day in his life. Everybody knows he's hiding out on his brother's farm outside of town for a reason. Illegal trade. Kayla might not want to be associated with him, but she can't escape her father's legacy forever. Besides, it's hardly fitting that she be crowned the winner of a contest when her father is a thief!"

"A thief?" I asked, from the passenger side of the car.

"Oh yeah. Steals from the common man." Deirdre paused. "Randy Wren is a common car thief. A kleptomaniac. I wouldn't be surprised if it ran in the family, you know. Regardless, Kayla's not the type of person who should win the grand prize and neither is Colton. Both of them would be terrible representations of—"

"We have to go," Lauren said, loudly. "We have places to be. It was nice to meet you." She got into the car and started the engine.

I followed her lead.

Deirdre hovered beside the car for a second longer, still talking as if we could hear her, before waving a hand and hurrying off to her car nearby. A black Prius.

Kayla and Colton had both left the Hungry Steer well before us, and I hadn't been able to glimpse their vehicles, unfortunately.

Lauren got us on the road before letting out a massive sigh. "I have never met a woman who talks that much. There's gossip and then there's whatever that was. Now, you know I don't like to talk ill of people, but good heavens."

"It was a bit much." But illuminating at the same time. Without having to interview either Colton or Kayla, I had discovered that both of them were poor, perhaps desperate for money, and Kayla's father was a thief.

It was good to have that information, but it didn't provide much evidence per se. Lauren and I drove through town in silence, her humming to a tune on the radio and me scanning the town's streets.

They were quaint with the road dividers containing flowers, grass, and trees. Wrought iron lamps populated the paved sidewalks, as well as cutesy benches. We entered Main Street and Lauren slowed, her window rolled down to let in the sweet night air.

Glass front stores, on the verge of closing for the night, provided snapshots into the lives of the residents. There was a young mother feeding her child at the diner, and a man doing some last minute shopping at the grocery store. Two elderly women talking over the counter in the antique shop and—

My eyes widened.

"Slow down, Lauren."

Thankfully, the chef obeyed instantly.

A couple sat on a bench up ahead. A tall, balding guy with a sharp-nosed side-profile— Brenda's boyfriend, Norman Sweet—and another familiar figure. Kayla Wren. The two sat arm-in-arm, Kayla resting her head on his shoulder.

They didn't notice us driving by.

The boyfriend of the victim with the poor, desperate Kayla? If that wasn't a dual motive for murder then what was?

Kayla needed money. Brenda may have had the recipe book. And Norman was supposedly the last one who'd been seen with Brenda.

The plot was custard. The thick, lumpy kind.

18

The following morning...

Lauren yawned as she prepared the key lime pie for after breakfast. She was in the habit of making something sweet for our guests every morning and this was great practice for the baking competition.

"Bad night's sleep?" I asked.

"It's difficult to sleep when you're the size of Wisconsin," she replied.

"Why Wisconsin?"

"First state that popped into my mind."

"We live in Texas." I scratched my temple.

"When I figure out how my brain works with all these hormones flooding it, I'll let you know." Lauren checked on her pie crusts in the oven. "Oh, that reminds me! Georgina asked to see you in the kitten foster center."

"Right. Be right back."

Lauren waved me off, yawning yet again.

I exited into the hall, pausing to stroke Sunlight and Cocoa Puff—both cats had set up camp outside the kitchen archway, dozing as they watched the morning activity. The door to the kitten foster center was ornate, carved beautifully, and kept locked at all times.

The only people who had the key were Gamma, me, and the new assistant who spent most nights in the center looking after the smallest kittens in the incubator.

I withdrew my key from the chain hanging around my neck and inserted it into the lock. One satisfying click later and I was in my favorite part of the inn.

The older kittens had free reign in the largest room, and they darted across the wooden floors, playing. A few of them scratched the cat trees in the corners, or used the litter boxes. My grandmother stood by the half-door that blocked the kittens off from the incubation room.

"Are you sure?" Gamma asked. "I'm happy to give you time off."

"I'm fine. I swear. I love it here." Our new assistant, Jemimah, sat in a chair next to the incubator, occasionally glancing at it to check on its occupants.

"Very well. Ah, Charlotte. I was hoping you'd come join me," she said. "Take a look at this." She led me to one of the rooms that had been part of the old museum. We'd kept it locked since we'd had no use for it after converting the place into the foster center.

Gamma unlocked the door and opened it. "I've remodeled the cat hotel!"

I gasped. The cat hotel, which had consisted of a corner in the kittens room where we'd kept the full grown cats away from the boisterous kitties, separated by a simple room divider, had needed an upgrade.

"This is amazing!"

The room, wide enough to accommodate several humans let alone cats, had been filled with all the amenities a cat away from home might need. Separate kitty sleep areas that were closed off from each other, an open play area, a feeding corner, and a place for the kitties to go potty in state-of-the-art litter boxes.

There were toys galore, and my Gamma had installed a TV on the wall that cycled between videos birds and fish.

"How did you afford this?" I asked.

"I don't pay myself a salary," she replied.

"That's not good, Georgina. You have to look after yourself."

"Spare me the lecture, Charlotte. I'm fine."

She beckoned for me to enter the new cat hotel room then shut the door behind me. "This isn't the only reason I wanted you to join me here. I wanted to touch base on what you've discovered."

I told her everything that had happened last night. "My plan is to investigate Kayla, and pay a visit to this Colton guy at the trailer park. He's a dark horse. I want to find out if he has an alibi for the time of Brenda's murder. Then I can focus solely on Norman and Kayla as my suspects."

"With the motive being the recipe book and unrequited love?"

"Exactly. If they believed the key lime pie recipe would land them the five grand from the competition..."

"I see your point," Gamma nodded.

"What about you?" I asked. "What happened last night?"

Gamma inhaled through her nose and glanced toward the lovely open windows that provided a view of the inn's grounds. "Nothing," she said, at last. "Nothing. Jessie spent the night with her husband and her guests." She pursed her lips. "And my FlyBoy Drone didn't find out anything interesting, other than Jessie wearing a pashmina to bed."

"You're kidding."

"I wish I was." Gamma walked to the window, folding her arms. "You stay the course, Charlotte. And I will too."

"Georgina."

"Don't try to stop me. I know Belle-Blue is up to something, and I'm going to find out what it is. You run along to that trailer park, Charlotte. I'll review the footage I have from the past week. I guarantee you, I'll find something of interest."

Why did that sound so ominous?

THE HAPPY CAMPER TRAILER PARK WAS situated on the outskirts of Gossip. A series of fields with plenty of trees, the trailers themselves bordered by grass. There were no tarred roads, but dirt created a center street that ran between the mobile homes. Most of them weren't mobile at all, but firmly seated on yellowed grass.

Gamma's Intel had provided me with the description of Colton's trailer—baby blue, rusted, and without wheels.

I found it at the end of the center road with several ornaments pegged into the grass outside the shoddy front steps. We didn't have much information on why or when Colton had decided to move in here, but according to the grapevine, he wasn't a very good tenant. Was he renting this mobile home?

I parked the Mini-Cooper and went up to knock on his front door. A few knocks nearly buckled it inward.

"Hello?" I called. "Is anybody home?"

"Hey. Hey, you there." The rasping voice had come from the trailer beside Colton's. It was a side fancier, sleek and cream colored with its windows open, providing a view of the neat interior. A skinny woman wearing a faux fur coat hung out of the window, her hair in curlers. A cigarette hung from the corner of her lip. "You looking for the freaks who live here? You want the tall one or the short one?"

"Hi," I said, retreating from the steps before they crumbled underneath me. "There are two men who live here?"

"Sure are. You want the skinny or the short one?"

"I'm looking for Colton Harrison. Is he home?"

"The tall guy, right? Blond with the facial hair?" She gestured to her chin. "Talks like a robot having a bad day?"

"I guess so," I said.

"Nah, he's not here, honey. But I'd stay away from him if I were you. Pretty girl like you shouldn't mess with trash like him. Just look at the state of this house." She gestured with her cigarette, and ash dropped to the grass. "The man's no good."

I brushed fingers through my short,

blonde hair. "He's not that bad," I said, trying to ham it up. Maybe I'd get some information out of this lady.

"Not that bad? He's up all hours of the night with that roommate of his, making noise, banging pots and pans. His house always smells too. Like burned sugar. Granted, I can't smell that good, but it's not a good smell."

"Do you know what car he drives?" I asked, fishing now.

If Colton drove a white Kia, as Misty had claimed she'd seen driving around the area on the morning of Brenda's death, I might have a lead.

"Oh, honey, no," the woman rasped. "No, he hasn't got any wheels. The man walks everywhere." She studied me, her eyes narrowing. "Listen, you want to come in for some tea? He works a lot of jobs so I don't know when he'll be back, but if you really want to waste your life on this man, I can keep you company until he arrives."

"Thanks for the offer, but I'd better get going. Do you know where he works?" I asked. "I'd sure love to go see him."

"Nah. I don't talk to the freak. Seriously, honey, don't waste your time."

"Hey," I said, before she dipped back inside. "This might seem like a weird question, but—"

"Weird questions are my bread and butter, honey, you go ahead and ask."

"Was Colton home early on Monday morning?"

"This last Monday?"

"Yeah."

"Well, darn, I don't know. I tend to sleep in," she said. "Why, honey, do you think he's cheating on you?" She dropped more ash onto the floor as she took a drag of her cigarette. "I wouldn't put it past him. Never trust a man who has cobwebs for a beard."

I thanked her for the help then headed back to my grandmother's car. There was nothing for me here, but that was fine. I had other leads to follow. Like the affair between Brenda's boyfriend and one of her chief competitors at the baking contest.

But first, I had my duties to attend to, and they were meant to come first, especially with the baking contest two days away.

❧ 19 ❧

I arrived back at the inn before 11:00 a.m. to find my grandmother waiting under our reconnaissance tree. She held her laptop and gave me a look that filled me with trepidation. She had found something. That or she had finally made good on her threats and set up a dating profile for me. Heaven forbid.

"I have interesting news," she said. "Take a seat, Charlotte."

"What's going on?"

"Firstly, I've had Jemimah scour the

grounds for any sight of animal tracks and there are none. No wolves in sight. It's exceedingly strange. And secondly, well, it seems that one of our suspects has been up to no good." Gamma paused, tilting her head. "Pardon me, no. Most of them have been up to no good, but this one in particular."

"Who?"

"Take a look at this. My cameras picked it up early this morning." She pointed toward the cameras situated atop the porch roof. They pointed down into the front yard, one directed toward the distant fountain and bushes and the other toward our bench.

"What is it? The suspense is killing me." I shifted closer to my grandmother and peeked over her shoulder at the screen.

Once again, video footage had been pulled up, but it wasn't Jessie Belle-Blue snooping around the inn this time.

Glendaree Bijon descended the front steps of the inn on the screen. She wore a silver kaftan, her gray tresses piled atop her head. She hurried off to *our* bench under the tree and sat down, a book on her lap. She opened it and began paging through it, frantically.

"This was taken this morning at about 06:00 a.m. when everyone was indoors and occupied," Gamma said. "What do you make of it?"

I squinted at the book on Glendaree's lap. "It's her recipe book, isn't it?"

"I'm not sure, but it sure seems that way. The only thing I don't understand is why she'd come read it out here and not keep it in her room."

"You mean the only thing you don't understand apart from the fact that she hired me to find a book that was never stolen in the first place," I replied, and hot anger flashed through my core.

Glendaree had acted strangely from the start. She was an outsider yet had known that I was Gossip's problem fixer. She had sought me out to find her recipe book and now, she had made a fool out of me. The recipe book had never been stolen.

"Take a breath, Charlotte," Gamma said. "We don't know whether this is true or not yet."

"It has to be. What else could that be?" I pointed at the book in Glendaree's lap on screen.

"Go find out." Gamma shut her laptop.

***

I KNOCKED ONCE ON THE DOOR TO THE Lavender Room before inserting a key into the lock and entering. As one of the maids, I had the keys to every room. I never used them to disturb guests, but this was an exception to the rule.

Gamma had stayed downstairs to help Lauren with lunch and to ensure that if the chef's water broke, she went to the hospital instead of staying to finish her baking.

"What is the meaning of this?" Glendaree

Bijon was at her dressing table, a book open in front of her. She slapped it shut and covered it with both arms, drowning it in her silver kaftan.

"Mrs. Bijon. I've come to talk to you about your case."

"My case? I assume you've yet to solve it," she replied, sniffing and tossing her head, but it was clear she was nervous.

I had hoped that the blurry image of the thick, hardcover book on Gamma's laptop had depicted a work of fiction, in more ways than one. But Mrs. Bijon's actions were transparent to me. She was trying to hide her recipe book.

The one that had been "stolen."

Be calm. Channel your grandmother's cool demeanor.

Gamma was the queen at handling tough situations, but this was infuriating. I had been lied to. Mrs. Bijon had already *paid me* the first half of my fee to find the recipe book that was in her possession.

"Well?" Mrs. Bijon insisted, trying to act

natural even while she lay half of her body over the book she was trying to hide. "What have you discovered? Why have you burst into my private space like this? I could report you to your employer, you know? I'm sure Georgina Franklin would be very interested to hear how rude you are and—"

"Why did you hire me to find a book that was never stolen?" Was it connected to Brenda's murder? Had she sent me over there to find Brenda's body, after planting that mysterious note mentioning the recipe book under the fridge?

But no, that didn't add up.

"I have no idea what you're talking about," Glendaree replied. "I hired you to find my stolen recipe book."

My patience vanished. I walked over to Mrs. Bijon, calmly reached beneath her arms and wrenched the recipe book out.

Glendaree let out a squawk of horror. "How dare—"

"Case closed." I held up the recipe book.

"Why, Mrs. Bijon, did you hire me to find this recipe book when you had it all along?"

"This is just... it's a copy of my recipe book," she said, clearly thinking on her feet. "That's all. A copy. I don't know who stole the original."

"Liar." I opened the recipe book. The pages were well-worn with plenty of Glenda-ree's personal notes in the margin. "Why did you do this?"

But Mrs. Bijon wouldn't talk. She clammed her lips shut and stared at me, blankly.

"And why did you take it outdoors to read it on the bench?"

Again, no answer.

"What was it, Bijon? Was it because you wanted to cast suspicion on Brenda, last year's runner-up? You wanted her to get in trouble for a crime she didn't commit? What was it?" My voice was loud in my ears, and Mrs. Bijon recoiled.

Calm down, Charlotte.

My grandmother's voice rang through my

mind. This wasn't like me. I had spent years staying calm under pressure. You couldn't be a spy without a tough skin, without assessing the situation at hand with logic and clarity.

I took a breath and dropped Mrs. Bijon's recipe book onto her lavender-frilled comforter. "I'm firing you as a client," I said. "I'll be keeping the upfront fee you paid me but you can keep the rest. I don't work for liars."

Rich coming from an ex-spy, sure, but this was different. She wasn't hiding out from a rogue spy. And her recipe book had been implicated in a murder case. Except she'd had it all along.

I gave Mrs. Bijon a final moment to tell me what was going on. She didn't. I left her at her dressing table staring into space.

20

Late that night...

"Back to the drawing board," I said, the minute I'd entered my grandmother's armory. We'd agreed to meet down here to discuss the recent developments in the case and in Gamma's conquest to find out what Jessie Belle-Blue was up to.

"You must keep calm." Gamma tapped away on her touchscreen desk, bringing up multiple tabs of information at once. "Calm mind, clear decisions."

"I know," I said. "I don't understand why I'm struggling with that so much lately."

"Because this case is the only thing you have at the moment apart from dusting the inn and serving guests who complain all day long," Gamma replied, without lifting her gaze from the screen. "I'm telling you, Charlotte, being a retired spy should be a paid gig. The amount of times I picture blow darting a civilian in the neck..."

I snorted a laugh.

"You're dropping the case," Gamma prompted.

"The case of the stolen recipe book? Yes. That's out of the window, but the murder case? That I'm interested in."

Gamma gave me a knowing look.

"What? There's not much else to do around here?"

"No one's disputing that." My grand-mother swiveled her chair, her arms folded over a neat cotton robe. She wore a pair of fluffy slippers that dangled off the toes of one foot as she sat, cross-legged. "But the point is, you want to know what happened. And I have some new information."

"You do?"

"Yes. As of this morning." Gamma swiveled again and tapped on the touchscreen desk. The image of today's newspaper headlines appeared.

Poisoning by cyanide!

"Their headlines are going downhill."

"Regardless," Gamma said, "our suspicions about the method of poisoning were correct. With this confirmation, I started doing a little research to help you."

"What have you found?"

"That cyanide isn't readily available as it might've been in Agatha Christie's novels. Not everyone has a medicinal cabinet in their home," she said.

"Right, OK. So what does that mean for us?"

"I cross-referenced the industries that use cyanide in their processes and found nothing nearby. There's only one place this cyanide could've come from, locally, assuming our killer didn't bring it from another part of the country when they came for the competition."

"And that is?"

"There's a chemistry lab over in Crabapple," Gamma said. "About an hour's drive to the South. That's the nearest place."

"Right, OK, so we have to find out if any of the suspects have been there? Or know someone who works there."

"My thoughts." Gamma acquiesced, bowing her head.

"But the suspects themselves are a problem," I said. "There's Glendaree who lied about the recipe book being stolen."

"She didn't just lie. She kicked up a fuss for two days prior to her approaching you, Charlotte. She wanted everyone to know she'd been wronged. But to what end?"

"I don't know. It doesn't make sense to me.

Was she doing it to disadvantage Brenda? Was that it? To make her chief competitor look bad so that when it came to the judging, she might be disqualified? Or was it something more sinister?" I paced back and forth, clicking my fingers at my sides. "And then there's Brenda's boyfriend, Norman. He was mighty cozy with Kayla last night."

"Kayla with a father who's been locked up for grand theft auto." Gamma tapped on the screen again to bring up a picture of a leery looking guy with dark circles under his eyes. "He's out now. Apparently, he's been repairing cars and is going clean."

"I bet Kayla and Norman worked together," I said. "Worked together to get rid of Brenda. But the note!"

"The note referencing the recipe book we assume was left by the killer."

"Who else could've left it behind? It seems obvious that the murderer brought the pie and water as a thank you for help with the recipe book. Which would implicate Glendaree." I stopped pacing. "Unless they were talking about a different recipe book? It didn't seem likely at the time, but we are about to host a baking competition in Gossip."

"Yes."

I let out a groan. "This is so frustrating!"

"Breathe, Charlotte, for heaven's sake. You're not cut out for this type of thing," she said. "You were a spy, not a detective. Think about it logically. Who was the last person seen with Brenda?"

"Rumor says the boyfriend, but there's no evidence of that. And then there's the mysterious white Kia that was seen driving around the block early on the morning of the murder," I said, and chewed on the inside of my cheek. "Glendaree doesn't have a car that we know of, but we never know with her, given that she hired me to find a recipe book that wasn't stolen."

"Bitter as burnt sugar," Gamma teased.

I did a double take.

"What?"

"Nothing. Nothing, just the way you said that reminded me of something. I don't know what." I counted my suspects off on my fingers. "So we have Kayla and Norman, Glendaree the liar, and then there's Colton Harrison who might have done it, but doesn't appear to have a car. Do we know what Kayla and Norman drive?"

"Norman drives a blue honda. Kayla's as much of a mystery to me as she is to you," Gamma said. "And I don't like that at all."

"You know what? You're right. We need to peel back a few layers on that relationship. If we can't get through to Kayla herself then I'll settle for talking to Norman about these new developments."

Gamma beamed at me. "Atta girl, Charlotte. That's the spirit."

❧ 21 ❧

I arrived at Norman Sweet's home on Brewer Lane at 09:30 a.m., having left Gamma to do the washing up with Lauren. Obviously, I had her permission to do so —she was still my boss. This case took precedence over dishes. The sooner we figured it out, the easier it would be to get back to normal life.

Is that so?

I got out of my grandmother's Mini-Cooper. Once again, Norman appeared to be home.

His screen door was wedged open, and the porch swing was still in motion, a glass pitcher of lemonade on the table beside it, beads of condensation dripping down its side. For a man who needed to leave early for work every day, Norman sure was home a lot.

"Mr. Sweet?" I called, broaching the front gate and starting up the path. "Mr. Sweet, are you home?"

A commotion started inside, a whispering and then silence.

"Hello? Mr. Sweet?" Two glasses next to the pitcher of lemonade, eh? Norman had company. "Hello?"

Finally, a figure appeared in the doorway. It was Norman himself, wearing a tank top, barefoot as he'd been the day before, this time with his blue jeans rolled up above a pair of bony ankles.

"Yeah?" He stopped, glaring at me through dark eyes.

"Could I talk to you for a second? I'm not

interrupting anything, am I?" I glanced point-edly at the glasses of lemonade.

"No." His reply came with a tone of childish defiance.

"No I can't talk to you? Or no I'm not interrupting anything?"

"No you're not interrupting anything." Norman joined me on the front path, looking as if he'd like to frogmarch me right back to the sidewalk but not daring to do it. A good thing too. It'd been a while since I'd broken a man's arm, and I didn't want to do it now.

"Mr. Sweet," I started.

"Now, what's this about?" he asked, before I could get to the point. "You can't just come by asking me questions at odd hours of the day. I've heard all about your reporter types, and I won't take it, you understand me?"

"Reporter? Oh, right!" I'd told him I was from an online magazine last time I'd been here. "Yeah. Well, it's 09:30 a.m. so I thought it would be an OK time to drop by."

"I might've been at work," he said. "What about that? Did you think about that?"

"I've been thinking about you a lot, Mr. Sweet, actually. I've been thinking about how strange it is that you moved on from your deceased girlfriend so quickly."

Norman made choking noises in his throat. "I—"

"There's no use denying it, Mr. Sweet," I said, going for the jugular. "I saw you and Kayla Wren together. And I'd wager that she's in your house, right now. So, are you going to tell me the truth about what happened?" I'd skipped through interrogation techniques, right to the confrontation. I was out of patience with these games, and I needed something that could link Norman to the crime.

"How—?" Norman trembled on the spot. "I don't care if you know."

"Excuse me?"

"I don't care who knows that I'm dating Kayla," he said, louder this time.

A figure appeared in the doorway of his house. Kayla herself, clasping the doorjamb, white as a sheet. "Don't," she hissed. "Please. Stop it, Norman. We agreed—"

"Enough, Kayla. I'm starting to think you're embarrassed of me or something."

"It's not that."

Then what was it? Why was Kayla afraid that her connection to Norman would be exposed? Was she worried about another detail being exposed, perhaps? That she had gotten close to Norman for another reason?

Now that the recipe book was out of it, I had to consider other reasons for why Brenda might've been murdered. That narrowed my suspect list down to those closest to her. Who had different motives.

"Look," he said, "look here for a second. I don't care who knows that Brenda and I were on the brink of breaking up. The woman drove me crazy. Day and night with books and recipe books and having friends over and helping people. It was annoying. I didn't want to be with her anymore. In fact, I planned on breaking up with her on the day it happened."

"But you didn't get the chance because someone had already taken care of that problem for you?" I asked, bluntly.

"How horrible." Kayla turned on her heel and fled into the house. An air for the dramatic.

"If you want to say that, then yes, I'll agree. Kayla and I have been seeing each other for months now, and we love each other. I'm going to marry her. There's nothing you or anyone else can say that will stop me now," he replied. "Nothing!"

A match made in heaven. Both over the top and strange.

"You've told me the truth about your relationship with Kayla. Will you tell me the truth about what you saw on Monday morning?"

"I did," he replied. "Not that I owe you anything! Dirty reporter. They always say never talk to the press, and they're right. I shouldn't have bothered."

"You told me everything you saw? You didn't notice anything suspicious next door?" I asked.

"No," he replied. "Brenda was asleep. The most blessed time of the day was when her mouth wasn't yapping away."

Isn't he delightful?

"Now, get off my property!" Norman took a threatening step forward.

"A final question, please, Mr. Sweet," I said. "Where do you work?"

"The library. Not that I owe you any answers." And off he marched back up the stairs toward the front of the house, calling for Kayla.

I left his front yard and walked across to the Mini-Cooper at the entrance of the cul-de-sac, trying to piece it together. If he worked at the library, why did he have to wake up early to leave for work? Unless he worked in more than one place? Did everyone in Gossip work multiple jobs?

I sighed, tapping the car keys against my palm, the soft whisper of the breeze in the bushes that flanked the yard behind me bringing no comfort.

🎕 22 🎕

"**P** *ssst!*"

I froze, my grandmother's car keys in hand. Had I just heard someone whispering? No, that had to be the wind in the bushes, right? I looked up and down the street, but it was empty. So now I was just imagining things.

Perfect.

"Psst! Over here!"

OK, I definitely hadn't imagined that. The voice, small and feminine had come from behind me.

I spun around, frowning at the hedge, trying to find the source of the voice. This had been a strange week. From the werewolf to the non-stolen recipe book and now this?

"Who's there?" I asked, feeling like I'd lost it completely. "Hello?"

The hedge rustled and two skinny hands appeared, pressing the leaves apart. A face followed. "Hi." It was Misty, the reclusive graphic designer who lived next door to the victim.

"Uh, hello," I said.

Misty's eyes darted from left-to-right as she scanned the road. "I didn't want to be seen."

"You don't say."

"Things have been scary around here the past few days. The police were here. The dead body. Then you came by, and now people in the street are acting mighty strange."

This might've been a redundant question regarding that statement but... "Can you give me an example? How have people been acting different?"

"Norman," she whispered, "has been having visitors over to stay for the night. A young woman. It's not right."

"Anything else?" It was obvious that the woman visiting Norman was none other than Kayla, a main suspect in the case.

"Remember how I told you that I saw a white Kia on the morning of Brenda's... on the time that... you know the day that...?"

"She passed?"

"Yes, the day that she passed." Misty wasn't aware that a stray ant had started its long journey across the pale expanse of her forehead. "A white Kia. On that morning."

"Yeah?"

"Well, I think I know who it belongs to."

"Who?" My vision tunneled on her. If she had the answer to this question, it might be my next big lead.

"That woman who moved into Brenda's house. Her sister. Marie Tippett."

"You're sure about this?"

"Positive," she whispered. "Absolutely sure. I mean, I saw her driving down the street in a white car. I saw it with my own two eyes, and I've been keeping a close eye on things since we talked." The woman's eyes were wild, so I'd have to trust they'd done their job.

"All right. Thank you for telling me this, Misty."

She shushed me frantically. "I was never here," she whispered. "We never talked." And then she slowly retracted herself from the hedge with a great deal of susurration.

As encounters in Gossip went, this one was right on target. I was interested in the information she'd provided.

Marie Tippett had been obvious about pointing out how she'd arrived after her sister's death. And how her sister had been a nuisance. She'd also been surprisingly calm about Brenda's passing.

It was time to find out what she was hiding.

"I AM ENTIRELY SURE THAT SHE'S GOING TO throw the competition. She must be up to something," Gamma said, as we crouched in the same hedge I'd encountered Misty in earlier in the day. "Belle-Blue has no issue stepping on people's heads to get what she wants."

"You don't think it's so she can get more visibility for her cattery and guesthouse? I don't like the woman either, but killing someone?"

Gamma pursed her lips but remained silent. She'd had a bee in her bonnet ever since she'd seen yet another article in the newspaper declaring that Jessie was a town hero for being a judge at the impending contest.

"Georgina, you don't really believe that, do you?"

"We should focus on the mission," Gamma murmured.

The night sky was inky black above us, the

streetlamps on, and many a living room window in the street colored with the blue flashes from TVs. It was still early, but now was our chance to break into Brenda's home.

Marie had left on foot a short while ago, her bag strung over her shoulder. We had no idea where she was going, and it didn't matter.

"Move out on my mark," Gamma said, her voice loud in my earpiece.

"Copy."

She made the signal, and we darted across the road like shadows. Or like two women wearing all black including balaclavas this time.

I hit the scrambler once we were on Brenda's property and we made for the garage this time instead of the back door. Gamma removed a small black remote from her pocket and placed it against the garage door, pressing buttons along its side. "One moment."

"What are you—?"

She hit a button and the garage door

opened by remote. I didn't bother asking how she'd done it. My grandmother had a pill, remote, and gadget for every occasion. Our night vision contact lenses saved us the necessity for flashlights.

The garage interior was small, and a single car was parked within, surrounded by shelving that held loads of junk.

"No wonder Brenda's house was so neat," I murmured. "She was hoarding everything in here."

"The car?"

I checked it out and my heart sank. It was white, just as Misty and Norman had described, but it wasn't a Kia. It was a sedan, nowhere near the same shape as a hatchback. One witness's testimony might've been a mistake, but two?

"I don't think it's the right car," I muttered. "And we don't know that she was here on the morning of the murder. It appears as if she only arrived after the fact."

This was a bust. A waste of a mission and our resources.

"Let's make a tactical retreat, Charlotte." Gamma backed out of the garage doors. "In and out before anyone sees us is fine, but lingering here…"

"I know. Just give me a second." I peered in through the windows of the car, hoping there'd be something. But no. The car was empty of interesting stuff. It was just a car. An old one by the looks of it.

"Charlotte."

"Coming."

We raced back across the road, and Gamma closed the garage door remotely. "What a waste of time," I whispered. "I'm sorry about that."

"Never apologize for finding a lack of evidence," she replied. "It simply means we need to do more digging. I'll do a background check on Marie Tippett. See what we can find. Now that we know the recipe book isn't connected to Brenda's death we can cast our net wider."

Which I probably should've done from the start. But hey, I was a spy not a detective. I was working with the evidence I'd found.

And so far... man, that wasn't much.

23

The night before the baking competition...

I tucked my feather duster underneath my arm and fished my small notepad and pencil out of my apron pocket. I leaned against a bookcase in the library, chewing on the inside of my cheek. Fifteen minutes from now, the first official ghost tour would begin, and I would help lead the guests through the spooky library part of the tour.

My costume—an undead maid—was meant to strike fear into the hearts of the guests, but I was struggling to concentrate on the task ahead.

I was stuck on Brenda's murder.

Hastily, I scribbled out my notes.

Glendaree Bijon lied about recipe book being stolen. No alibi.

Norman Sweet had ample motive to get rid of Brenda, but claims he was going to break up with her. No alibi. Supposedly works at the library but leaves for work early? Very suspicious.

Kayla Wren wants to win the competition and was canoodling with Norman Sweet. Find out alibi?

Colton Harrison wants to win the competition but doesn't have a strong motive. Find out alibi?

Marie Tippett supposedly arrived after her sister's demise. Can't be a suspect then, can she?

White Kia or hatchback sighted near house on morning.

Muddy bootprints on the front porch but the flowerbeds were dry.

Note under the fridge that mentioned the recipe book.

Brenda invited a lot of people over and was friendly.

Potential attempted murderer on the loose? Could that be the reason why none of this makes sense?

"Charlotte." My grandmother poked her head around the library's heavy oak wood door. "Are you ready?"

"Yeah." I slipped my notepad and pen into the front pocket of my apron and brushed off my hands.

"Good. You look frightful!"

"As per the plan." I'd done my makeup white and ghostly with dark circles under my eyes.

"Lauren is leading them from the kitchen. They'll be here any second." My grandmother's excitement was palpable, and I couldn't fault her for that, even though I was utterly frustrated by the case and my lack of progress.

You should've focused on getting their alibis be-

fore anything else. But it was easier said than done. People weren't willing to talk to strangers about their whereabouts.

A knock rat-tatted at the library's door, and I drew myself up straight. I had practiced my lines for tonight over and over again. Spooky stuff was my favorite, especially with Halloween in a couple of months.

"Enter," I said, lifting my chin, and sweeping my feather duster through the air.

The library door creaked open—Gamma had decided we'd forgo oiling the hinges to add to the creep factor—and the guests and attendees of the ghost tour shuffled into the library. A few of them gasped at the sight of me, and I swallowed my mirth.

"Welcome, living ones," I said, with another sweep of my feather duster. "I have a horrid tale to tell. Will you listen? Or will you flee?"

A younger teen in the back let out an audible gulp. Her friend nudged her and rolled her eyes.

"Answer me," I yelled, drawing several shocked cries. "A simple yes will suffice."

A variety of responses in the positive followed.

"Very well." Another sweep of my feather duster as I strutted toward a bookcase. "You have entered the library of the Gossip Inn, once a museum, and before then... who knows what this building was used for? Rumor has it that the original owner was a recluse. A hermit. And all who stepped onto these grounds would suffer a fate worse than death."

I paused, allowing the words to sink into the room. They were, of course, untrue. Gamma and I had no idea how the inn had come to be. Even the previous owner of the museum had been unsure of its history.

But for the sake of the ghost tour, we used a variety of tall tales to feed the fear. After the murders that had occurred at the inn, it was easy to draw in a crowd of people driven by morbid fascination.

"He installed a variety of secret passages,

one of which would lead to a guest's ultimate demise." I leaned over and clicked the button on the side of the bookcase. There was a click, and it swung outward, revealing the rickety staircase beyond.

The ghost tour attendees gasped. The teens murmured appreciatively.

"Now, it's getting cool," a girl whispered.

"Follow me," I hissed, and started up the stairs.

The guests shuffled in behind me, a deathly silence descended upon them. At the top of the stairs, we entered the attic. Gamma and I had discussed putting up a recreation of the scene, but we figured it was a little too soon to do that. It was one thing to host a ghost tour, but we didn't want to mock the deceased.

The attic itself was spooky at this time of night. We'd set up several lanterns to cast their flickering light across the collection of covered and uncovered furniture, most of it dusty.

"In this very room," I said, walking to the end of the attic and stopping beside one of the windows that looked out on the roof's shingled overhang and the inn's grounds below, "a man was murdered. Strung up and left to die. It is rumored that his spirit haunts the attic and library, roaming across it, occasionally letting out a scream of terror to frighten those guests who—"

A piercing howl broke through my words.

The ghost tour attendees yelled, screeched and grabbed onto each other.

It would've been priceless if not for the fact that the howl wasn't part of the script. I had a recorded scream that I could play from my phone at any moment, and I had *not* touched the button.

"What was that?" a woman cried. "Did you hear that?"

"It's not real. This is not real."

"I'm totally freaking out right now, Dorothy. Are you totally freaking out right now?"

"We're not in Kansas anymore, sister."

While I appreciated the humor in the *Wizard of Oz* references, it didn't help clarify what on earth was going on. This wasn't part of the plan.

I glanced out of the window, and my heart went cold.

A wolf paced around outside in the grounds, right beside the greenhouse. It let out another howl to the inky night sky. The guests rushed toward the windows, gasping and pointing.

"What's that?"

"It's a wolf! A werewolf!"

"Don't be ridiculous, Dorothy, werewolves don't exist."

"Didn't I tell you we weren't in Kansas anymore?"

"I thought you said you were from Arkansas?"

Another figure appeared near the greenhouse. This one, a woman wearing a cloak.

No. A pashmina.

Belle-Blue! Caught in the act. Why had she brought a wolf to the inn's grounds? Had Gamma been right about her all along? Was she somehow involved in what had happened to Brenda or...?

Another person appeared below. My grandmother. Marching toward Belle-Blue.

"Everyone remain calm," I said, and then I dropped the feather duster, popped the window open and climbed out of it onto the roof.

The guests screamed. They applauded. They would surely be back again for round two. Heaven only knew how I'd involve this in the routine the second time around.

Agile as a cat, I moved down the roof tiles and toward the drop off to the first floor overhang above the kitchen door. I dropped down onto it, then let myself off the edge and onto the steps.

"—knew you were up to no good!" My grandmother's voice carried across the grounds.

"No idea what you're talking about," Jessie said. "I'm out for a stroll, that's all."

"With a wolf?"

"This is a husky," Jessie replied.

I rushed across the grass toward the pair. My grandmother faced off the pashmina-draped interloper, her fists on her hips. The wolf, actually, a beautiful blue-eyed husky that barked and hopped, occasionally letting out a howl, seemed fascinated with the greenhouse.

"You're spying on us, aren't you?" Gamma asked. "You knew tonight was the first night of the ghost tours so you decided to come by and see what information you could gather."

"Your ghost tours pale in comparison to mine. Now, if you'll excuse me." Belle-Blue tried walking off but Gamma caught her arm.

"You're not going anywhere."

"Unhand me, you witch!"

"Hey," I snapped at the pair of them. "Calm down. Belle-Blue, if you don't want to get arrested for trespassing, I suggest you tell us what you're doing here. Now."

"I told you. I was going for a stroll." Belle-Blue folded her arms. "Clearing my head before I judge the baking competition tomorrow." Even now, caught trespassing, the woman was insufferable. She cast a smirk at my grandmother. "Aren't you happy for me, Georgina? Judging a prestigious competition like this?"

"You're up to something. I'm going to find out what it is."

The husky sniffed and whined, letting out another howl and scratching at the greenhouse door. What was that about?

"Charleston," Jessie said, patting her leg. "Charleston, come here, boy."

The dog ignored her. I didn't blame him.

"Charleston!"

I glanced back up at the attic window. Most of the guests had their hands and noses pressed to the windows, watching in awe as the situation unfolded.

"I'm calling the cops," Gamma said. "How about that, Belle-Blue? I bet they'll be very interested to hear you've been trespassing on my property for the past week. Oh yes, I know all about it. I have camera footage. They call that direct evidence, you know. Direct evidence of your crime."

Jessie paled.

The dog yelped and whined.

My irritation at the situation grew, and I marched over to the greenhouse door and opened it with a thunk.

Three things happened simultaneously.

Jessie screeched for me to stop.

The husky dog let out a yip of glee and streaked into the greenhouse.

And a man, standing in the center of the greenhouse wearing ragged clothes, a smiley face tattoo underneath his eye, turned and tried to run out of the back door of the greenhouse.

Except there was no back door. He slammed into the misted glass at the back and broke through stumbling before crashing to the ground face first.

"It's the convict!" I said. "Quinton McLarkall." I raced out after him, crunching over broken glass. The husky dog rounded the side of the greenhouse, avoiding the glass, thankfully, and licked the side of the man's face.

Quinton groaned. He had several small lacerations on his cheeks.

"Quinton!" Jessie screeched, and ran over, flapping her pashmina like a bat from the below. "Quinton, are you all right?"

"I'm fine, auntie."

"Auntie?" Gamma and I asked in unison.

"What's the meaning of this?" Gamma asked, striding over. "Why are you here? Belle-Blue?" The danger in her tone struck fear into my heart, and I wasn't on my grandmother's bad side. "Explain yourself!"

Belle-Blue rolled Quinton over and checked him for serious wounds, fussing and cooing.

"I'm fine," Quinton said. "I didn't get injured. Just a few cuts and scrapes. Sorry about your greenhouse."

"Jessie." That was all Gamma had left to say.

Belle-Blue's chin wobbled. "I didn't know where else to bring them. His father kicked him and Charleston out of their home after Quinton was released from prison and I can't have them at the guesthouse. I... I can't do it."

"Why not?" I asked.

"Because she's afraid of how it will look," Gamma answered instantly. "You didn't want to ruin your chances of being a judge for the Tri-State Baking Competition, isn't that right, Belle-Blue?"

The other woman nodded mournfully. "I needed a place where Quinton and Charleston would be safe until the competition was over. Everyone in this town is so judgmental! Even though he's been proven innocent, they still think that he killed that man."

"I didn't," Quinton grumbled. Charlston

had crawled into his lap and was licking his face, wagging his fluffy tail like crazy.

"He's my only blood relation left," Jessie said. "His mother passed, and his father is an evil creature who married into our family. I just wanted to keep him safe."

It was the first time I'd seen a soft side of Belle-Blue, and I didn't like that I felt sympathy for her after all the trouble she'd put us through.

"And you thought you'd use my inn as a safehouse? My greenhouse?"

"He only sleeps here at night," Jessie said. "It hasn't been a problem until now. It—"

"Quiet." Gamma raised a hand. "I should have you both arrested for trespassing."

Quinton bowed his head. Charleston, who was growing cuter by the second, whined and wagged his tail at us.

"But I won't. Belle-Blue, you're going to pay for the repair of my greenhouse. Quinton, you can stay here, in the shack on the edge of the grounds. You'll pay your way by helping with the gardening. Charleston can stay too. Outdoors. Nowhere near my cats."

What was my grandmother thinking? I was all for empathy, but what if this guy was a murderer?

If he is, it will make questioning him that much easier.

"Thank you," Quinton said.

Jessie looked like she'd swallowed a toad. She didn't like relying on my grandmother for anything, but what could she say? The alternative was losing her spot on the judging panel due to negative public opinion.

"I don't like this one bit," my grandmother continued, "but that's the way it's going to go. And once the anger and fear have blown over, Quinton, we'll discuss next steps. Perhaps, you'll move in with your aunt then, though I don't see why you'd want to when she's made it clear she's embarrassed by you."

Jessie colored and opened her mouth to say something, doubtlessly snarky, before snapping her jaws together.

"Quinton," I said, the thought occurring to me. "Where were you on Monday morning?"

"I was with my aunt," he replied, nodding to Jessie. "She took me to Crabapple to get breakfast."

"It's true." Jessie's tone was displeased.

Would Jessie lie to protect Quinton? Or was that a stretch? It seemed he had an alibi for the morning of Brenda's murder and that meant that this was yet another dead-end in the case.

24

The following morning...

The day of the Tri-State Baking Competition had arrived. The stage was set, and the final round of judging was in progress.

A massive marquee tent had been set up in the Gossip park and the judges, including Jessie Belle-Blue in a maroon pashmina, stood atop a grandstand, waiting as the finalists gathered beside them, carrying their cakes, pies, and cupcakes.

Only five had made it through to the final round.

Gamma had decided to stay home because she couldn't stand the sight of Belle-Blue up on the stage. I waited in the audience, cheering as Lauren waddled up the steps, assisted by another of the contestants, and took her place beside one of the pedestals.

I'd never been more proud! She'd made it all the way through with her rendition of key lime pie, even though she'd been convinced that she should drop out of the race.

"And now, it's time for the final judging." An anchor from a local news station had been hired as the host of the contest. He wore his hair in a blond coif and it wiggled each time he lifted his microphone to announce something. "Our finalists are tense as they wait for the judges to try each of their offerings."

Belle-Blue and the two other judges, people whose names I hadn't absorbed when they'd been announced, approached the first of the contestants.

Glendaree Bijon had prepared a sumptuous red velvet cake and had chosen a matching red velvet kaftan for today's outfit. She fluffed her gray curls and stood back, watching the judges as they tucked into her cake with a smirk.

"She really thinks she's going to win this," I muttered, shaking my head.

"Huh?" The woman beside me leaned in, but I merely shook my head and smiled at her. A flicker of movement within the tent caught my attention.

Kayla Wren and Norman Sweet stood nearby, talking deeply and looking decidedly unhappy. A lover's spat? Or was it just because Kayla's meringues hadn't done her any justice during the first round of judging? She hadn't made it through.

"Delicious," Belle-Blue announced, her voice broadcast by the mic attached to her pashmina. "I've never tasted a red velvet cake this moist."

"The buttercream frosting is smooth but a little on the heavy side," the second judge said, smacking his lips.

Glendaree looked at him as if he'd sprouted a tail and a pair of horns.

"I agree. Moist cake slightly sullied by heavy buttercream." The third judge was a young lady who wore a cream blouse and had a sniffy air about her. "Try cream cheese frosting next time. There's no need to reinvent the wheel when making a red velvet, even for a competition like this."

Glendaree choked on her saliva and barely managed to thank them for the critic. Challenging them would likely end with her receiving even worse scores.

The judges moved down the line to the next contestant, Colton Harrison, the hardworking trailer-dweller. He grinned at them, stroking his goatee as they announced that he had produced a near perfect scone with cream and homemade strawberry preserves.

"An interesting entry," Belle-Blue said, adding hardly any value to the proceedings. Good thing Gamma wasn't here—she might've heckled her.

Again the judges moved on. They gave out their judgments and made both positive and critical remarks, all while the audience lapped it up, making the appropriate oohs and aahs when something was said.

Finally, they reached Lauren's pedestal.

"Not my cup of tea," Jessie said, seconds after she'd taken a bite of Lauren's key lime pie.

I nearly saw red. She was trying to sink our chef just because she worked at the Gossip Inn. Trust Belle-Blue to do something like this. The audacity! And after Gamma had said that she would hide Quinton at the inn too? I would go up there and—

"I disagree," the second judge said. "I think this is perfect. Crust is divine, the filling is just right. There's a touch of something in there that I don't recognize but it truly uplifts the flavor."

"Meringue is sweet and fluffy with the crunch on top. Oh yes. Wow. Amazing." That from the third judge.

Lauren, who had wilted at Belle-Blue's critic, beamed at the judges now. "Thank you so much. It's my own recipe, I—"

"Trash!" The shout had come from Glendaree at the end of the stage.

Everyone gasped and looked over at her. The judges turned as well.

"Mrs. Bijon, please don't interrupt the judges while they are—" the host started.

"She stole that recipe from me!" Glendaree declared. "She stole it from my recipe book. Didn't you hear that my recipe book was missing? She stole it from me." Glendaree grasped a bottle of water in one hand swinging it back and forth as she talked. "I demand that this thief be disqualified, immediately."

"Mrs. Bijon!" The host's cry was strangled,

but he glanced toward the cameramen, ensuring that they got a close-up of the interruption. This made for good TV.

I glared up at Glendaree. She was ruining this for Lauren.

Glendaree took a deep swig of water from her bottle before continuing, "If you think that I, as last year's esteemed winner, will stand to be judged against a petty thief who can't even create her own recipes for this competition, you are—" She choked and dropped the bottle. Water splashed across the stage.

The audience members gasped and shouted.

"Mrs. Bijon, you are disturbing the judges. This is against the rules." The host strode toward her.

Glendaree didn't hear. She pressed a hand to her chest. She slid that hand up over her kaftan toward her throat and sucked in a shuddering breath, her eyes bulging. Her cheeks reddened.

Uh oh.

Glendaree Bijon took a stumbling step forward. Her eyes rolled back in her head and she collapsed on the edge of the stage. Dead as a doornail.

Screams erupted in the tent. The host looked this way and that, seeking aid from heaven alone knew wear, his blond coiff bobbling. Lauren sat down heavily, gasping for air and faint at the sight of Glendaree's body.

Chaos.

Pure and utter chaos.

Remain calm. Gamma's voice in my head. My internal compass, always there and ready to guide me. *Look for the killer.*

Because they had to be here. I scanned the crowds of people, some caught in horror staring at Glendaree with morbid fascination, others on the phone, trying to get through to 911, and some in dead faints or in varying states of distress.

Not Kayla Wren. She tugged free of Norman's grip, staring at Glendaree's body, and then ran for the exit.

"Stop her!" I yelled, but my voice was lost in the chatter. "Stop her! She's getting away." I had never been more certain that Kayla Wren had set this up. She had murdered Brenda for a book that hadn't been stolen and then done the same to Glendaree when she couldn't make it to the finals. "Stop her!"

I pushed through the crowd, chasing after Kayla, but her mousy brown hair disappeared in the crowd.

My pulse raced, and I pumped my arms back and forth trying desperately to catch up with Kayla before it was too late. I burst from the crowd and headed for the park's entrance, but it was too late.

Kayla Wren was gone.

25

"At the scene of the crime again, I see." Detective Goode made the comment as he passed me by. He didn't stop to continue taunting me, but made for the now cordoned off marquee tent. "You've got a knack for finding trouble." That was thrown over his shoulder at me.

I gritted my teeth as he strode away, my arms folded. I didn't give him the courtesy of a reply, partly because he struck me dumb—a first for me—but mainly because I had other places to be, and arguing with him would only delay me.

"Thank you, ma'am," the police officer said, and handed me his card. "If you think of anything else, you can feel free to call this number. We're setting up a tip line related to today's event. You think of anything else, you call, OK?"

"I've already told you who did it," I replied. "So why would I call the—?"

But the officer had already moved onto the next of many witnesses. I was free to leave the park now that I had given my statement about the events that had unfolded just over a half an hour ago.

Glendaree dead. Poor Lauren in a state. And the judges announcement postponed until they could rouse Belle-Blue from her faint. Of course, she had passed out in front of everyone a good ten minutes after Glenda-ree's death. Typical Jessie.

My phone buzzed, and I extracted it from my pocket.

Around the corner. Big G.

A text from my grandmother. I exited the park, checking that no one was on my tail, and hurried around the corner.

My grandmother's Mini-Cooper was parked across the street. I got into it, a wave of adrenaline lifting me from my irritation at Detective Goode.

"What have you found out?" I asked.

"Kayla is on the run," Gamma replied, starting the engine but waiting for me to put on my seatbelt. She tore down the road, dodging pedestrians with professional driving maneuvers. "She's not at Jessie Belle-Blue's guesthouse. Was last seen packing her bags and rolling them down the front path."

"Ah. The actions of an innocent person." I'd known that she had to be involved in this. She'd had an affair with Brenda's boyfriend, for heaven's sake. And the first thing she did was run for it? "Do we know how she's getting out of town?"

"No. She doesn't have a car," Gamma

replied. "And that leaves us but two options. Firstly, that she leaves via bus or secondly, she runs to her father's home."

"The thief."

"Correct. I'm taking us to Mr. Wren's home." Gamma put the car in high gear and we flew down the streets, taking corners with precision and terrifying several of the locals who were used to a more leisurely style of driving in Gossip.

Mr. Wren lived on a farm, except instead of fields of crops, he had one field that was filled with cars and car parts.

Gamma parked her Mini-Cooper in front of the farmhouse, a broken down wooden building that looked as if it'd fall over in a stiff breeze, and we got out, squaring our shoulders.

"No sign of her," I muttered.

"Don't give up hope yet, Charlotte."

We walked up the front steps of the farmhouse, the wood creaking dangerously underfoot, and knocked on the front door.

Silence, and then.

"Who's that?" A gruff voice from within.

"Mr. Wren? Can we talk to you for a moment, please?" Gamma called, sweetly.

"Who is it?" He wrenched the door open, and I held my breath. He smelled strongly of bourbon and cigarettes. I glanced down at his shoes for posterity, but he wore a pair of trainers that were pretty small. I doubted they'd match the size of the prints I'd found on Brenda's porch.

"Mr. Wren," Gamma said. "Hello. My name is Georgina Franklin."

"I heard of you," he replied. "You run that inn where all those people keep dying."

"We prefer the phrase 'murder hotel' to inn," I said.

Mr. Wren sniffed, not finding my interjection all that funny. "Yeah, and so? What do you want?"

"Is Kayla here?"

"Kayla? Heck no she ain't here. My daughter don't come visit me anymore unless she want something. Cut from the same cloth as that good for nothing mother of hers."

"When last did you see her?" I asked.

"Look here, now what's this about?"

"A car," I replied because I couldn't think of anything else that would be relevant to this man.

"Ah. Kayla's car?"

Gamma and I exchanged a glance. Had I just accidentally hit the jackpot?

"Kayla had a car?" Gamma asked.

"Well, sure, she used to have a car before she sold it to me. She had herself a white Kia, but it didn't work too well until I fixed it up. I offered to sell it back to her, but she wanted to keep the money rather than have the wheels. Strange if you ask me."

My heart did flip-flops. So close. This was all adding up. The white Kia!

"When did she sell you the car?" Now that we'd exposed the thread, I needed to tug on it.

"Oh, shoot, like a month ago? It sat on my lot for ages."

Wait, what? She sold the Kia a month ago, yet... huh? I don't get it. If Kayla hadn't been driving the Kia, then who had?

"I'd sell it to you," Mr. Wren continued, flashing us a yellow-toothed grin, "but I already sold it last week. Finally moved that piece of trash on."

"You did?" I asked.

"Who did you sell it to?" Gamma put in.

"I dunno. Some short, ugly lookin' guy. Young."

"What was his name?"

"Eh, let me think." Mr. Wren scratched his chin, the stubble rasping noisily. It took a painfully long time for him to access the memory centers of his brain. "Right, yeah, it was Brian something or the other. You'll have to ask Kayla. She was the one who gave him my details to buy the car. Some friend of hers or the other."

I made a mental note of that, but the name didn't ring a bell.

"He works out in the other town, but he

lives here in Gossip. Said something like that. He wanted a daily driver. A car that could put the miles in so he could get to and from work."

"Oh, uh, OK," I said. "Thanks, Mr. Wren."

"You really had your sights set on Kayla's old Kia, eh? Sorry I sold it. Might've gotten a better price from you." He let out a wheeze of mirth. "But, eh, no use crying over spilled gas. Might as well light a match to it and watch the world burn."

"In keeping with your aesthetic," Gamma said.

"Sure." He didn't seem to realize she'd insulted him.

"Mr. Wren, do you have any idea where we can find Kayla?" I asked, but as soon as the words had left my mouth, it hit me.

Of course! Norman Sweet.

Where else would she run to than his house? She'd probably hide out there until the coast was clear to make a break for it.

"No idea where she might—"

"I think I know," I said, turning to Gamma. "I know where she is."

"Then why'd you ask?" Mr. Wren called after us, as we raced back down the collapsing stairs toward the Mini-Cooper. "Hey, you looking to flip that car? I could make a tidy profit on that! Mini-Coopers are hot, nowadays, you know."

Gamma and I bundled into the car and took off, leaving Mr. Wren in a cloud of dust.

🦢 26 🦢

"What in the name of everything sweet and delicious is she doing?" Gamma asked, hands on the steering wheel as she peered out of the window up at Brenda Tippett's house.

Kayla, our mousy-haired suspected murderer, had climbed across Brenda's porch swing and was trying to worm her way through an open front window. The hem of her blouse had caught on window's latch and she let out a fitful cry every other moment, kicking her heels frantically.

"I think she's trying to break into the victim's house," I said.

"Good heavens. We're really scraping the bottom of the barrel for murderers these days, and that's saying something."

"She can kill two women with cyanide but she can't break into a house," I remarked.

The sense of urgency I'd felt earlier had waned, mostly because Kayla was well and truly caught—both in the act of breaking and entering and just in general.

We got out of the car and walked over to the front yard, frowning. The garage door was open, and Marie Tippett's white car was gone.

Gamma and I entered the front yard and clomped up the steps together, stopping behind Kayla.

Our suspect kicked her legs one last time then stilled. "Hello?" she whimpered. "Who's there? Norman, honey, is that you?"

"No," I replied.

"What are you doing, Miss Wren?" Gamma asked.

"Who is that?" Kayla was stiff now, trying to turn and catch a glimpse of us.

"Ready?" Gamma asked.

I nodded.

She stepped forward and unhooked the hem of Kayla's blouse. I grabbed our suspect and hauled her out of the window by her ankles. She came out with a yelp, two thwacks of her stomach and chin against the porch swing, and a groan once she landed on solid ground.

"Let go of me," she said, struggling against my grip.

Gamma removed two cable ties from her purse. She casually slipped one over Kayla's ankles and pulled it tight, before gesturing to me to grab her arms and secure them.

I did so, all while Kayla yelped and whined and accused us of kidnapping.

"Quiet," Gamma said, once she was secure.

We lifted Kayla from the floor and set her, upright, on the porch swing. "What are you doing to me? I'll scream! I'll scream!"

"I said be quiet." Gamma gave her the

stern, "scare the life out of you" look. Man, I had to practice that in the mirror. It was so effective. "Kayla Wren, we're aware that you ran from a crime scene today without giving your statement to the police. Now, we've found you breaking into the first victim's home. You may consider this a citizen's arrest."

"No!" Kayla cried, shaking her bound wrists at us. "Please! I didn't kill anyone. I didn't!" Her blue eyes went round and filled with tears. "I promise I didn't. It was... oh no, this is so terrible."

"Explain," Gamma said, brusquely. "You have thirty seconds before I call the police to arrest you."

"I-I-I think it was Norman!" she wailed. "I think Norman killed Brenda, but I didn't want him to get arrested because I love him and I just love him so much and I—please! You have to understand that I would never... I didn't want to... I think I'm going to be sick!"

"You're becoming hysterical," Gamma

said, bending to catch her gaze. "Calm yourself. Why do you think it's Norman?"

Kayla blubbered wordlessly.

Gamma calmly raised a finger and flicked the center of her forehead. "I said calm down."

Kayla swallowed her tears, immediately. Another trick I ought to know. Was there some pressure point in the forehead I hadn't learned about? Or was this just another of my grandmother's persuasive tricks?

"I didn't kill Brenda, and I didn't poison Mrs. Bijon. I saw the news about the cyanide, and I—" She took a breath. "Norman."

"Start from the beginning," I said.

Kayla nodded, licking her lips. "Norman and I started dating about two months ago. He was still dating Brenda, but things weren't going well between them. Norman didn't like working with her, so he started a job at the local store with me. I haven't had anywhere to stay since I lost my apartment and he kept trying to convince me to live with him. He said the minute I agreed, he would get rid of Brenda."

"Those were his words?"

"Yes. He said he would get rid of her," Kayla said, her bottom lip quivering. "But I didn't think he was capable of murdering her. I figured someone else did it, you know? But then... well, this morning I woke up and I found this recipe in his kitchen."

"A recipe?"

"Yes, it was a key lime pie recipe from Mrs. Bijon's recipe book. She had titled it 'Glendaree's Famous Award-winning Key Lime Pie Recipe' and I just knew that he must've stolen it. I confronted him about it but he denied it. He said he had no idea where it came from," Kayla replied. "We've been fighting about it all day, even at the contest. It was so bad that I couldn't focus on making my meringues."

"What happened then?" I asked.

"Norman kept on denying that he stole her recipe from her book," Kayla said, "and he asked me why I'd even think he'd steal it because he wasn't interested in baking at all. That had been Brenda's thing." Kayla sucked in breaths, the tears still in her eyes, but the panic at bay now. "I kind of believed him until Glendaree threw this big tantrum on stage and said that her recipe for key lime pie had been stolen. And then she dropped dead! I was terrified. I thought that Norman had... that he'd done it for me. That he had killed Brenda the same way because he wanted me to win the competition so that he could have the prize money. So I ran back here, and I..."

"And?"

"I'm not proud of it but I was going to hide the Mrs. Bijon's recipe in Brenda's house because I figured that was the first crime scene and if they found it there, it wouldn't seem that out of place, and it would mean that... Norman wouldn't get into trouble for trying to help me and win the money." A sob escaped Kayla's lips. "He's so awfully poor and he struggles to hold down a job. I just wanted to help him like he tried to help me. But now I'm more sure than ever that he's a murderer twice over and this is just terrible. It's terrible and evil and..."

"So, you didn't kill Brenda?" I asked.

"What? No! I wasn't even here on Monday morning! I was at Jessie Belle-Blue's guest-house. You can ask her. She'll tell you the truth."

If she'd let us get a word in. But now that we were looking after Quinton, Jessie owed us, big time. We could confirm the alibi. I glanced at Gamma who gave a nod, purse-lipped. She retreated a short way, pulling her phone from her purse to call Jessie and confirm the alibi.

Kayla watched her, tearfully. "You have to believe me," she said. "I wouldn't hurt a soul. I didn't want to... I just—the recipe."

Inside Brenda's home, lying on the floor, Glendaree's recipe, ripped from her book, lay on the floor.

So, someone had stolen the recipe from her. Not the entire book. Just the recipe. Unless, she had planted this herself? But how? And why? And why hadn't Glendaree told me that specific recipe had gone missing? And when had it been torn from her book?

I cast my mind back to the day I'd confronted her. She'd been paging through her recipe book in her room, somewhat frantically. Had that been the day she'd discovered the recipe missing?

Too complicated.

"Please," Kayla whispered, seemingly losing steam. Thank heavens for that.

"Kayla," I said. "Who's Brian?"

"Huh?"

"Brian. The guy you sold your car to. What's his name and who is he?"

The change in topic appeared to jar her. "H-He's a friend of mine from high school," she said. "Brian Stokes."

"I need to talk to him," I said. "Do you have his number?"

"Uh, yeah. On my phone, I think. It's in my pocket."

THE CASE OF THE KEY LIME CRIMES

I removed her phone from her jeans and found Brian's number, then copied it down. There was something more to this that we hadn't yet uncovered. Some third party working against us. I didn't buy that Norman had murdered Brenda, alibi or not.

And anyone at today's event would've had a chance to poison Glendaree's fluid. Someone there had killed her, and I got the feeling that Brian and the white Kia would lead us to the real murderer.

"Alibi checks out," Gamma called.

"Then let's go," I said. "I know what we need to do next."

"Hey, wait a minute." Kayla squirmed on the porch swing. "Wait, you can't just leave me here."

"Never fear." Gamma made for the front gate and I followed her. "I've called the good detective. He'll release you. I suggest you tell him everything you've told us. And don't mention our names, Kayla, or I'll be forced to pay you another visit." She smiled up at the detained young woman and patted her purse. "There's more than just cable ties in here."

"Has anyone ever told you you're terrifying?" I asked her.

"A few mass murderers and terrorists," Gamma replied.

27

Brian had agreed to meet us in a public place, namely, the Java Nother Day in Paradise coffee shop off Main Street. He'd been alarmed by how insistent I'd been but had caved when I'd said it was about Kayla's car.

Apparently, it wasn't working as well as it should have.

Gamma cruised down the street, her tires splashing through the water that had gathered from a busted pipe. "When are they going to fix this?" she asked. "It's been over a week, for heaven's sake. Look at this waste of water."

The entire street was wet, and the center divider was muddy from being splashed by passing cars. I frowned, something pinging in the back of my mind, but dismissed it as Gamma navigated to an empty parking space across from the coffee shop.

She switched off the car's engine then turned to me. "So, any idea what Brian looks like?"

"You mean apart from short and ugly, according to Mr. Wren?" Another ping in the back of my mind. A memory. Someone else had told me a man was short and ugly, recently. But who?

My brow furrowed.

"What is it, Charlotte?"

"I'm not sure. But something about this... something." I shook my head. "Anyway, Brian said he'd be wearing a red collared shirt, and he'd meet us outside the coffee shop in five minutes."

"Early is always better. If he's the one who drives the white Kia, it might've been Brian outside Brenda's house on the morning of her murder. Better to observe from afar at first."

Gamma was right, and again, there was something about what she'd said.

I scanned the street and spotted a short, squat guy wearing a red collared shirt across the road. He was outside the coffee shop, as planned. "That must be him," I said.

Another man emerged from Java Nother Day In Paradise and strode over to meet him. They put their heads together and talked, the second man gesturing down the street.

The second man was Colton Harrison, the baker who lived in the trailer park, and who worked a lot of jobs. Including one at the coffee shop.

A series of revelations slapped me right between the eyes, so sharp and fast, that I sucked in a rattling breath.

"Good heavens, Charlotte, what is it?"

"It's them," I said. "Look. Colton the

baker. He was one of the finalists at the contest, remember? One of our suspects." The words poured out of me. "When I went to the trailer park to talk to him, I encountered his neighbor. She told me that he lived with a short, ugly guy. I'd bet anything that the short, ugly man in question was Brian. Brian who bought a white Kia from Kayla! The same white Kia that was seen outside Brenda's house."

Gamma whipped her phone out and started typing into her internet browser.

"And the water! The mud. Look!" I couldn't stop now that I'd started. "Look at the mud, Georgina. You said this pipe has been busted for over a week?"

"Yes." Gamma was still furiously typing away.

"That water has flooded the center divider where there's grass. And mud! No wonder the killer's boots were muddy. The sludge from here must've stuck to his boots. He entered the yard, not from the road, but from one of the neighbor's yards to avoid leaving muddy prints on the sidewalk, but he still left them on the porch. And the flowerbeds were dry at Brenda's house. The mud didn't come from there. It came from here. From outside the coffee shop! I bet the inside of that Kia is covered with the stuff. It's got to be them. One of them. Both of them. I bet this is a trap! They thought they could lure us here and... but how did they get the cyanide? That's the only question."

"I know how," Gamma said, and showed me her screen. Brian's professional profile, including his image, job description, and place of work were listed. "Lab technician at Park Labs in Crabapple. The only place for miles where someone could get their hands on say, potassium cyanide salts?"

I balled up my fist and struck the dashboard. "It was them. Together. Oh my word, that neighbor lady of their's said that Colton was weird. That his house smelled of burnt sugar at odd hours of the night. I wonder if she meant bitter almonds? Or if she mistook the smell? Maybe they were experimenting with something."

"They're looking around," Gamma said. "Duck down."

We lowered ourselves in our seats. "This is a trap," I whispered. "They were going to talk to us here. Maybe poison us?"

"Maybe. Broad daylight in the coffee shop, though? Messy."

"I don't get it. What's in it for them? The money? Is that it?"

"I believe so," Gamma replied. "Think about it, Charlotte. Colton has taken out his main competition. Last year's runner-up and winner of the Tri-State Baking Competition. He likely banked on there being a lack of qualified entrants this year."

"For five grand? He killed two people for five grand? It seems unbelievable."

"Desperate men and women have killed for far less than that," Gamma said. "To them, it probably seems like the perfect crime."

Brian, complete with collared red shirt, lingered outside the coffee shop for another fifteen minutes, pacing back and forth, checking his watch, clearly frustrated by the situation. Colton watched from within, occasionally popping out to check on his friend and stroke his ridiculous goatee.

"Amateurs," Gamma said.

"Murderers," I put in. "I wonder if Goode has any idea."

"If they're this disorganized, this obvious about their intentions, then I'd like to think that he has some clue as to what they're up to. He's likely still gathering evidence. Investigations take time, Charlotte, especially when you're bound by the confines of the law."

"I see what you're saying." A sharkish grin parted my lips.

These young men had no idea what they'd done or who they were dealing with.

"Tonight?" I asked.

"It's not even a question, Charlotte." My

grandmother matched my smile with one of her own.

Gamma waited until Brian had left before starting the Mini-Cooper and driving us back to the inn to prepare for this evening's "festivities."

28

The trailer park was alive with noise at this time of the night. Dogs barking, the occasional burst of laughter from the trailer next-door, and the constant background noise of a TV from across the dirt road. Evening had just set in, and our targets had yet to arrive home.

Which suited us just fine of course.

My night vision contact lenses adjusted to the quickening darkness with ease, keeping the rusted blue trailer clear. Gamma had positioned herself in the bushes, but spoke clearly through my earpiece.

"I have the FlyBoy in the air above you, watching the road," she said, quietly. "No sign of the target yet."

"Copy, Big G. Moving in for data collection." I slinked toward the side of the trailer, my body armor breathable, flexible, and impenetrable. I loved the feeling of being in this gear. Being active sure beat dusting around the inn and waiting for something to happen.

"Chaplin," my grandmother said, using my code name, "I've got eyes on an entry point on top of the trailer. Sun roof. It's open."

"Copy that." I removed two suction cups from my utility belt and attached them to my gloves. With much less dexterity than my grandmother, I climbed the side of the trailer, using my arm strength to pull me up. Once on top of it, I removed the suction cups and perched like an over-sized black cat.

The coast was clear. For now.

I breached the sun roof and dropped into

the interior of the trailer, silently. The space was cluttered and smelled of sweat and cookies, oddly enough. The combination was stomach-turning.

"What do you see?" Gamma asked.

"Clutter. Somebody needs to read a Marie Kondo book."

"Ooh, I love her."

"Me too," I said. "And nothing about this trailer is bringing me joy." I moved through it, prepared to check cupboards and hack into a laptop if I had to. Turned out that wasn't necessary. "Imbeciles," I muttered.

"What is it, Charlotte?"

"They've left a portion of Bijon's recipe book out on the counter." I removed a button camera from my pocket and took several images of the pages that had been torn free. "Why? Just to frame Norman?"

"Probably. They're sloppy."

"I want answers."

"You'll get them, Chaplin. Target is on the

main road. You have three minutes to hide. I'll be joining you."

"Copy that, Big G." I searched for a hiding spot, my breathing calm, heart rate even. It was strange, but whenever I was in my spy gear, working with my grandmother, nothing could unsettle me. But when I was in the inn...

A matter for a different time.

I opened the sliding door of the bathroom and entered, closing it carefully behind me. The space was cramped, but there was a shower with a shower curtain.

I left the sliding door open a crack.

The crunch of tires on dirt came seconds after I'd hidden myself. A car door slammed then another.

"—panic," Colton said, in that snappy tone I'd heard at the Hungry Steer, the first time we'd met in person.

"I'm not panicking," Brian whined. "I'm just saying, don't you think it's kind of weird she didn't show up?"

"It's better this way. She's just some maid. She probably doesn't know anything."

"Shush! Somebody might hear you."

"Who? That old bat next-door?" Colton snorted. The trailer's door slapped open and heavy footsteps entered. Lights switched on in the main section of the trailer, and I kept back, listening as the pair moved around inside.

"I still don't like it, man. I don't like that we got that call so soon after that woman kicked the bucket."

"I'm moving to the roof, Chaplin. Maintain your position," Gamma said, in my earpiece.

"Copy," I breathed.

"Kicked the bucket?" Colton laughed. "You've got to upgrade your vocabulary, Brian, if you want the money, we've got a couple more people to take care of."

"Huh? You can't be serious. More? I didn't sign up for this, Colt. You told me you needed help and there would be a payday, not that I'd wind up just... murdering—"

"Shut up!" he hissed. "Don't say that word."

"Oh, now we can't talk about it?"

"We can talk about it. But don't say *that word*," Colton hissed.

A silence followed. Shuffling. Footsteps. "What do you want to do about these recipes?" Brian asked. "If somebody finds them, we'll get in trouble."

"I'll keep them for the next contest I enter," Colton replied. "In the next town."

"I don't want to do this again."

"Yeah, you don't say, but you didn't really think five grand would get us far, did you?" Colton asked, laughing. "Listen, you want to survive? Stick with me, kid, and we'll go far."

"You mean on a killing spree? We didn't have to kill that first lady. She didn't do anything."

"She should've given me that recipe book when I asked for it," Colton replied. "She made a mockery of me when she gave me the wrong book. Thought she was making a big joke, didn't she?"

"Maybe it was a mistake."

"Oh come on. Brenda stole the recipe book. She had to die," Colton snapped.

"But we never found the recipe book there. Bijon had it in the coffee shop. So maybe Brenda didn't steal it and—"

"You don't know what you're talking about!"

I tried piecing together what the two goons had said. They'd killed Brenda because she'd given Colton the wrong recipe book. Clearly, Colton had asked her for the recipe book and Brenda, who hadn't stolen anything, had mistakenly given him a random recipe book, likely from the library.

And Colton had taken offense to that.

They saw Bijon in the coffee shop with the recipe book. Likely, they either stole it from her there or ripped the pages out when she wasn't looking.

It was probably as close as I'd get to the

truth without questioning the suspects myself. Which brought me to the next phase of the operation.

"I'm on the roof, Chaplin," my grandmother said. "But we've got a problem."

"We've got two of them to deal with down here."

"This is a unique problem. Unique to our circumstance. Two patrol cars are headed down the dirt road, their lights flashing. I believe Detective Goode might be driving one of them."

So, Goode had figured it out without my help this time. Though, technically Kayla had given them information after we'd detained her.

"Abort the mission, Chaplin. I'm leaving the roof." My grandmother, who had been as silent as a cat up until this point, ran across the roof, feet thumping heavily.

"What the heck?" Brian cried.

Police lights flashed outside.

The bathroom didn't have a big enough

window for me to squeeze through. I was a sitting duck here.

"The cops!" Colton yelled.

Quickly, I detached the scrambler from my utility belt and hit the EMP button. The pulse took out the lights in the camper and fried my connection to my grandmother, but it would have to do. I rolled the bathroom door open and stepped out into the camper.

"The lights!" Brian shouted.

"Who's that? There's someone in here!"

I ignored the murderers and sprinted into the kitchenette. I jumped onto the nearest counter, then grabbed the lip of the sun roof and hauled myself out and on top of the trailer, lying low. I rolled off the side of the vehicle and dropped down behind it, hidden from Goode and the cops.

"This is the police," a man shouted. "Come out with your hands up."

Yeah, I didn't want to be here for this. Goode had caught up with Brian and Colton, and the murderers would be caught and locked up for good. It wasn't as clean as the last mystery we'd solved, but we'd helped. Whether the detective liked that or not.

I darted into the bushes and ran for it, my arms pumping back and forth. Gamma emerged beside me, and we ran together, keeping an even pace until we finally reached the SUV.

Once inside, we put on our seatbelts, and my grandmother started the car.

"Charlotte, I believe we'll be receiving another visit from your beloved Detective Goode, shortly."

"He's not my beloved," I replied.

"I was being sarcastic."

I cleared my throat, a blush creeping toward my cheeks. "I know."

"Of course you did." She patted my leg and winked.

29

Three days later...

The end of summer had arrived, and with it, had brought a day that was too hot for comfort. How could the start of fall be signalled by a day that was fit for the underworld? For Hades? I got off the rendezvous bench—I'd wanted a time-out outside to avoid what was going on inside the

Gossip Inn—and sweated my way toward the front steps of the building.

I paused on the porch, folding my arms.

You're seriously going to let a man keep you out of your own inn?

Detective Goode was in there conducting a final interview with Lauren. They had everything they needed to convict the goons, Colton and Brian, but he was tying off loose ends.

Just go inside. You're not going to run into him.

I hovered on the threshold, considering it. If I ran into Goode, would it be so bad? It wasn't like he could accuse me of anything. And, heavens, I didn't care if he smelled great or looked like a crabbier version of an Abercrombie and Fitch model, or—

Detective Goode appeared at the end of the hall, and I tried darting out of sight, but there was nowhere to go.

"Miss Smith," he said, from a distance, and I froze, wavering between darting down the stairs into the front yard and diving into the flowerbed.

Dignity! What would Gamma think?

"Goode," I said.

"I'm glad you're good." He emerged onto the porch. "Nice to see you again."

I didn't say anything, biting down on the side of my tongue instead.

"You know, I'm starting to think you really like cable ties."

"Excuse me?"

"Cable ties. Ah, come on, Smith. You don't think I'm that dumb, do you?" Detective Goode asked, in that smooth, seriously attractive drawl. Did I have problem? Why did I like arrogant men?

No. You don't like him.

"I have no idea what you're talking about."

"Sure, you don't." He took a step closer to me, and the heat of the day went up about twenty notches. "I believe I told you to keep your cute button nose out of my cases."

"And I believe I told you... uh, goodbye," I said.

"Smooth."

"Whatever." I made to walk past him and he caught me by the wrist, his grip firm and warm.

"You know, one of these days you're going to crack," he said, "and ask me out on a date. I'm just letting you know that I'll have to refuse. I don't date."

I pulled my arm free. "Yeah, you flatter yourself enough all on your own. Don't let the door hit you on the way out, Goode." I entered the inn, redder than a sun-ripened tomato.

"I'm already outside," he called after me. "How would the door hit me if I'm already outside? Huh? Hey, Smith, I'm talking to you!"

I ignored him, grinning to myself, even as my heart pitter-pattered away at the memory of his touch.

Silly woman. He's not worth your time. That

was my internal voice rather than the one who sounded like Gamma.

I entered the kitchen and found Lauren preparing a pitcher of lemonade. "Isn't it the hottest day?" she asked, stroking her belly. "I mean, talk about the end of—oh!"

"Oh?"

"It's nothing," she said. "Just a Braxton-Hicks thingie. Contraction. They're fake contractions, you see?"

"Fake contractions? Lauren, are you sure they're not—?"

Lauren's phone rang, and she hurriedly retrieved it from the kitchen table. She answered it, ignoring me even as she frowned and touched a hand to her belly. Gamme joined us, stopping to stroke Cocoa Puff and Sunlight in the doorway on her way in.

"The detective has left, I see," Gamma said. "You've decided to end your self-imposed banishment?"

"It wasn't about him. I just needed some fresh air."

"And I need to have a tea party with Jessie Belle-Blue. See? We're both liars."

I rolled my eyes like a teenager.

"No!" Lauren shrieked, her face lighting up. "Are you serious? You can't be serious? Are you serious? No! Yes?" She squealed and threw her phone up in the air.

"What's going on?" Gamma asked.

"No idea."

The phone dropped onto the tiles and shattered, but it didn't affect Lauren's good mood. "I won!" she shrieked. "I won the Tri-State Baking Competition! My key lime pie recipe won! They're going to have a prize-giving next week."

"Wow, that's amazing, Lauren," I said.

"Fantastic. I knew you had it in you." Gamma applauded. "We'll have to celebrate. We'll—" Her eyes widened, and I followed her line of sight.

A large pool of water had appeared underneath our chef. "I won! I won!" Lauren danced on the spot, completely unaware of what had happened. "I won! I won! I won! I—what? What is it?"

I pointed at the tiles.

Lauren looked down and colored pink. "Oh. I think my water just broke."

"I'll call Jason," Gamma said.

"I'll clean the kitchen," I offered.

Lauren blinked then grasped her stomach, groaning, "And I'll have a baby."

TEN LONG HOURS AND ONE KITCHEN scrubbed from top to bottom to prevent a visit from the local health inspector later, the nurse permitted us into Lauren's private room at the hospital. She sat up in bed, holding her little bundle of joy wrapped in a pink blanket. Her cheeks were flushed, her red hair in disarray, but her smile was so wide I couldn't help but grin back at her.

Jason sat in a chair beside her, Tyson fast asleep on his chest. The little Tyke, as we loved to call him, was tuckered out after waiting hours for his sibling to make an appearance.

"There you are," Gamma whispered. "Is she sleeping? I'm assuming it's a little girl?"

"Yes," Lauren whispered. "We've named her Rebecca. I'm so glad you came!"

"It's good to see you ladies," Jason said, rather stiffly. I doubted it was good to see us. We'd never liked Lauren's husband overly much. "I'd better take Tyke home to rest. We'll see you in the morning, honey." He kissed Lauren on the forehead, then little Rebecca too, before heading out of the room.

"How was it?" I asked, softly, and took the seat he had vacated.

The hospital room was decorated in pinks and creams, and Lauren looked positively radiant in the setting. "Grueling," she said. "But worth it. Same as the last time. Would you like to hold her?"

"Me?" I pointed at my chest.

Gamma gave me an encouraging nod. "Go on, Charlotte."

"You're an auntie, now," Lauren said. "At this point, we're basically related, Charlie."

"Thank you." I took the baby carefully, supporting her little head, and instantly fell in love. She was a warm lump in my arms, one tiny hand with five perfect fingers thrown above her head. Her mouth sucked in her sleep then settled. "She's gorgeous."

"Isn't she?"

"I can't believe it," I whispered, admiring the little girl. I'd always thought Tyke was cute, but I hadn't been there when Lauren had given birth to him. This was different.

Rebecca was tiny and precious, and a fierce need to protect her settled over me.

"See, Charlotte? There's more to life than gun battles and bringing down bad guys," Gamma said. "Perhaps you should start a family of your own."

"Yeah, sure," I said, but my usual sarcasm was lacking. "I'll get right on that."

Gamma took the baby from me, gently, and rocked her back and forth. "Now, of course, you'll have to take time off work. I'll need to find a replacement for you until your maternity leave is done. I'll pay you for the time, naturally, Lauren."

"Thank you, Georgina. I've got to say, winning the competition came at the perfect time. Jason's been struggling at work and..."

The background noise of their conversation dropped away. Another baby had been born in Gossip, and whether I'd planned it or not, I *had* a family. Lauren and Gamma, Rebecca and Tyke. With each passing month, I became more and more ensconced in this slow-moving life.

And I loved it.

I loved living a boring life in Gossip. I didn't want to leave.

I just wanted to figure out how I fit in.

But that was a question for another time. Now all that mattered were my cats, friends, and family. And definitely not that handsome Detective Goode.

Charlie and Gamma's adventures continue in The Case of the Custard Conspiracy. *Get you copy by clicking this link.*

CRAVING MORE COZY MYSTERY?

If you had fun with Charlie and Gamma, you'll want to meet Milly and her pet bunny Waffle. You can read the first chapter of Milly's story below!

"It's unheard of! A travesty." My grandmother, Cecelia Pepper, sat on the edge of her seat at the coffee bar in the Starlight Cafe. "Why, the sheriff ought to be ashamed of himself. How are we meant to walk down the streets in this town with this... threat in the backs of our minds? Looming! Like some giant Sword of

Damocles over our heads." She tapped the newspaper, a copy of *The Star Lake Gazette*, she'd laid on the coffee bar the minute she'd sat down.

My grandmother was the definition of dynamite in a small package. At 75-years-old, she was brimming with vigor to make up for her height.

"I'm sure Sheriff Rogers will figure it out." I fixed Gran a cup of coffee—a hazelnut latte with extra cream—and placed it in front of her. "It's a small town, Gran. They'll catch whoever's doing this."

"A small town that's going downhill quickly." My grandmother glanced around as if she was afraid of someone overhearing our conversation.

But the painful truth was there was nobody in my cafe this morning. Just like there'd been nobody in it the day before.

As I'd learned quickly, folks in Star Lake, Iowa, were insular. They didn't care that my late father, a town favorite, had left me the cafe. I hadn't lived in town long enough for them to trust me, and then there was the fact that I had absolutely no experience in the hospitality industry.

Not now. Just take a breath and smile.

"I mean, really. A mugger? Here? Nancy from the bakery told me her sister's best friend's cousin was attacked. Wallet stolen. Can you believe that? If I didn't love the lake and the people so much," my grandmother continued, lifting the latte, "I'd move away in a heartbeat."

"Gran."

"I'm serious."

"Gran, you've lived here for thirty-five years."

"Fine. I might not move, but I'll protest this at the next town council meeting. You can mark my words on that." Gran took a sip of her latte, pressed her lips together and fluttered her eyelashes. "Nearly as good as your father used to make."

A silence ensued, filled with our shared

sorrow. It was too soon to talk about him.

I cast my gaze away from Gran and studied the interior of the cafe. Light streamed through the windows and the glass front doors, illuminating the linoleum that was in need of a revamp, as well as the checked tablecloths and laminated menus. The chairs were comfortable and well worn. The cash register was an antique and the walls were dark wood.

Overall, the aesthetic was typical of my dad's taste. Hastily thrown together but with plenty of heart.

"This really is good." Gran must've noticed the lump in my throat. Metaphorically, of course. "You know, you'll make a fine restaurant owner. As fine an owner as you would've made a detective."

That was another touchy subject. "Thanks, Gran." I forced a smile.

She reached over and patted my forearm.

Movement outside on the brick-paved sidewalk caught my attention. A homeless woman, wearing a shabby coat and carrying several plastic bags, walked up and took a seat outside the cafe.

"Oh dear," Gran said.

"Do you know her?"

"Only by sight," Gran replied. "She's new to town I think. I'm not familiar with her story. Poor woman."

I bit down on my lip then headed back to the coffee machine and started fixing another latte. Much to my surprise, the bell over the door tinkled, and Sheriff Rogers entered.

He was in his late fifties, with a gray mustache, balding, and wearing his uniform with pride. He sauntered over to the bar and eyed me. "Morning."

"Good morning, Sheriff," I said. "What can I get for you today?"

The sheriff didn't immediately answer me. He scanned the interior of the cafe then pointed over to a new section I'd set up, with the help of my cook, Francesca. "What's that?"

"That's the waffle station," I said, smiling. "Do you want to try it out? We prepare the waffles fresh, bring 'em out to you, and then you decorate them as you see fit. There's ice cream and maple syrup, there's—"

"That wasn't here when Frank was running the place."

"No," I said. "No, it wasn't. I figured that people would enjoy—"

"Waffles?"

"Sheriff Rogers," my grandmother said, and the sheriff jumped a little.

"Celia." He sniffed, using Gran's nickname. "Shoot. I didn't see you there." And he sounded truly regretful, like he was anticipating a volley of complaints. He wouldn't have been wrong in that respect.

"What's this I hear about a mugger?" Gran tapped the newspaper. "A mugger in our midst?"

"Well, yeah, there have been reports of muggings over the past week, but I assure you it's under control."

"Now, Sheriff, you know better than to shovel that level of manure around me," Gran said. "I want answers, and I want them now. What am I supposed to tell the ladies in my book club? That we can't walk to the library in peace?"

"I assure you..."

The conversation faded out as I finished off the latte, grabbed a cupcake from the display of about a dozen under the glass counter, and walked out into the sunlight.

It was the end of summer, the weather a temperate 70 degrees with a soft breeze brushing down the street. I stopped in front of the homeless woman.

"Good morning," I said.

She glared at me, her skin tan, and her ire obvious. "What do you want, Red?"

The urge to brush my fingers through my red hair nearly overtook me. Thankfully, my hands were full. "Uh."

"Let me guess. You want me to move. It's a free country, you know, I—"

"No," I said. "I just wanted to check if you were OK."

"OK?"

"Yeah." I handed her the coffee and the cupcake. "You need anything?" It was my experience, after working as a beat cop in the city, that everyone had a story. Just like everyone had a purpose. Sometimes life just... got in the way.

The woman blinked. "Uh. Yeah. I'm good. Thanks."

"Sure. Just holler if you need a glass of water or something," I said. "I'll be inside."

The woman, still full of mistrust, nodded then took a sip of her coffee. I headed back into the cafe and found Gran and Sheriff Rogers embroiled in their argument.

"—muggers on the streets. If you think that we'll stand for this then you're delusional. You know, I can call up the heads of the three factions, right now, and get them to arrange a meeting."

Sheriff Rogers, blustery as he was, paled at that.

The "factions" as they were called, were the three unions that pretty much ran Star Lake. There were "the boaters", "the butchers", and "the bakers"—and they frequently disagreed on issues, to the point where the town was practically split into three. It was expected that you'd fall into line with one of the groups even if you weren't an active member of said union.

"The bakers would be most interested to hear about your lack of action when it comes to crime on our streets. I mean, this whole area is packed with bakeries and restaurants. This is bound to affect tourism too. And then the boaters will get antsy."

The summer months in Star Lake were famed for their fun boating activities, from tours on the lake, to fishing, to jet skiing and recreational activities.

"You're complaining about mugging and crime on the street," Sheriff Rogers said, finding his voice, "yet you won't stop your granddaughter over here from feeding said criminals."

Gran jerked back as if she'd been slapped —a strange effect on a tiny woman in a floral-print dress. "Feeding them? I think the heat is getting to you, Sheriff."

"She just took out a coffee and a cupcake to..." He trailed off and gestured toward the homeless woman now sitting on a bench out front.

"And so?" Gran grew red and rose from her barstool, trying to tower at four feet eight inches.

The sheriff tugged on his collar. "All I'm saying is that if you don't want trouble, don't invite it into your home." And with that, he swept from the cafe, trailing his overbearing spicy cologne.

"Idiot," Gran muttered.

"Gran."

"There's no love lost between us." She resumed her seat. "And for good reason."

But she didn't go into the reason. I fixed a cup of coffee for Francesa, who was in the kitchen, patiently awaiting orders that would likely never come, and then joined my grandmother at the counter.

Gran paged through the newspaper, stopping on an image and tapping it. "See, now, this is why you don't want to get on the wrong side of those boaters. Look at that. A full page ad for their 'Boating Blowout 2021.'"

I read over her shoulder. "Join us for a boating extravaganza as we celebrate the end of summer."

"You're going, I assume? Everyone's going," Gran said. "Everybody who's anybody. It will be a great opportunity for you to network, dear. It's been a year, and you've only made one friend."

"Thanks, Gran."

"I'm just saying," she replied, "that it might be a good opportunity for you to get out there and meet someone."

"Meet someone? The only person I'm interested in meeting is an accountant who can help me manage my finances for this place." Things were *not* looking good. And I was *not* about to let down my father's legacy by losing the Starlight Cafe.

"I'm sure there are plenty of eligible accountants around."

"Not what I meant, Gran."

She gave me a sneaky smile, and it cheered me up. I couldn't stay mad at Gran.

"Are you coming by tonight for supper?" Gran asked. "I'm making chicken casserole. You can bring Waffle along."

"That sounds great."

It sure beat eating a microwave dinner over the kitchen sink.

Want to read more? You can grab **the first book** in *THE MILLY PEPPER MYSTERY SERIES* at your favorite print book retailer.

Happy reading, friend!

PAPERBACKS AVAILABLE BY ROSIE A. POINT

A Burger Bar Mystery series

The Fiesta Burger Murder

The Double Cheese Burger Murder

The Chicken Burger Murder

The Breakfast Burger Murder

The Salmon Burger Murder

The Cheesy Steak Burger Murder

A Bite-sized Bakery Cozy Mystery series

Murder by Chocolate

Marzipan and Murder

Creepy Cake Murder

Murder and Meringue Cake

Murder Under the Mistletoe

Murder Glazed Donuts

Choc Chip Murder

Macarons and Murder

Candy Cake Murder

Murder by Rainbow Cake

<u>*A Milly Pepper Mystery series*</u>

Maple Drizzle Murder

<u>*A Sunny Side Up Cozy Mystery series*</u>

Murder Over Easy

Muffin But Murder

Chicken Murder Soup

Murderoni and Cheese

Lemon Murder Pie

<u>*A Gossip Cozy Mystery series*</u>

The Case of the Waffling Warrants

<u>*A Mission Inn-possible Cozy Mystery series*</u>

Vanilla Vendetta

Strawberry Sin

Made in United States
North Haven, CT
28 July 2022

21950808R00171